Finding the Way Back

Marcie Shumway

A New Reality Publishing
South Paris, Maine

Finding the Way Back. First Edition.

Published by A New Reality Publishing, 54 High Street, South Paris, ME, 04281.

Visit our website, www.ANewRealityPublishing.com, for more information on other *Reality: It's All In Your Mind*™ materials and to view the full line of our books and products.

Cover design and book layout by Christopher S. Harris, A New Reality Publishing.

Original cover photography by Jessica Woodcock, Lost in Reverie Photography

ISBN 0692919074
ISBN13 978-0692919071

Table of Contents

Finding the Way Back
Marcie Shumway

Acknowledgements

This is always the part of the book that I struggle the most with. I never want to leave anyone out, and words are never enough to let each person know what they mean to me. As I close this series, I want to tell anyone I haven't mentioned before now know that I appreciate them. Even those with the smallest part in my journey.

First and foremost, I need to thank my husband. He has always pushed me to keep chasing this dream of writing my books. On my worst days, he made sure that I kept going. Justin, you are my forever, and I love you.

Next, I need to thank my publishing company, A New Reality Publishing and the owner, Christopher Harris. He and his wife, Jen, have been the two that have helped me to get my name out in the indie world and for that, I will forever be grateful.

Jessica Woodcock of Lost in Reverie Photography, my books wouldn't be what they are without your gorgeous pictures gracing the cover. The friendship we've developed through this series still amazes me, and I will always treasure it.

My muses, you wonderful group of ladies, I couldn't have finished these books if it hadn't been for your never ending feedback and comments. The text messages and emails always made me smile.

Thank you to the Murphy's for the use of their beautiful front porch on a miserable rainy day. I truly appreciate you welcoming us onto your property to shoot to our heart's content. The cover wouldn't have been complete without it.

Lastly, I cannot give enough credit to Kristyn and Kyle Stebbins for agreeing to work with us on the cover. The weather was miserable, and I had been struggling with writing the book. You two kept smiling for us and gave me a better picture of my characters. Thank you!

About the Author

Marcie Shumway has been writing short stories for others to enjoy since she was in middle school. Finding the Way Back is the final book in her Finding Series. It is the fourth book she was published. She is an avid reader who thrives on the many books of her favorite authors.

Marcie resides in a small town in Maine with her loving husband. The two share their home with their cat, Kyzer, and their dog, Dani. They also have two horses, Chance, and Dee.

<u>Chapter 1</u>

The room was white, so white it was blinding. The smell of antiseptic permeated my nostrils causing my stomach to turn over. My heart started pounding so hard I thought it would explode from my chest. I needed to get out, and I needed to do it fast. Slipping from the room, I dodged nurses and doctors and rushed down the hall to the staircase. Reaching it, I pulled open the door and hurried down the two flights to freedom. Thankfully the stairs were near the front door, I burst through them sneaking past an older couple on their way in. Now, I could breathe.

Gulping in fresh air, I closed my eyes and let the sun beating on my face and the spring breeze blowing my hair calm me. It wasn't long before I heard the soft *whoosh* of the doors. I caught the smell of woodsy cologne, and I knew Kyle had come out. He gently uncurled my fingers from the fist I wasn't even aware I had been making and intertwined his with mine. He didn't say a word, just stood there with me.

Tears of frustration pricked the backs of my eyes. I felt selfish, and I didn't like it. I wanted to be there for my friends, celebrating their joy. Instead, I couldn't help but be wrapped up in my own problems. Feeling a tear run down my cheek, I fought the sobbing that wanted to come with it. Kyle came around in front of me and pulled me into his arms. Wrapping one arm around my shoulders, he tangled his hand in my hair and brought my face to his chest. I inhaled his strength, warmth, and the familiarity that was my husband and ran my hands up his back.

Finding the Way Back
Marcie Shumway

"I love you, Samantha," he whispered after a few moments of us holding each other.

"I love you more," I replied lifting my head enough to kiss the hollow part of his neck that was showing above the collar of his long-sleeved t-shirt.

"Why don't you go get in the truck, and I'll tell everyone good-bye," he suggested pulling the keys from his pocket.

I hated sending him back in the hospital to bail for both of us when we should have been spending hours there with everyone. I started to shake my head, but he lightly touched his fingers to my chin to stop the motion. Taking one of my hands in his, he dropped the keys in my palm and kissed my forehead before pushing me towards the vehicle while he headed inside. I let out a sigh and kept walking without looking back.

Unlocking the Dodge, I opened the passenger door and used the handle to pull myself up. Once I was safely inside, and it was running, I felt the tears flow more freely, and I let them. This time I didn't try to stop the sobs that tore from my chest or the wet trails streaming down my face. I pulled my knees up and buried my face in them. Before I knew it, strong arms were pulling me across the seat and into a solid muscular lap and chest.

Being in this man's arms just caused me to cry harder. Kyle Hart had always been my rock. We had been together since high school and had married as soon as we had graduated. College hadn't even put a damper on our relationship, yet these days I didn't know where we stood. I couldn't figure out what was going on in my own head, never mind what was going on in our marriage. Squeezing him as tight as I could, I released another round of heavy sobs and fat tears.

Finding the Way Back
Marcie Shumway

I'm not sure how long we sat there like that, him holding me in his lap like a little kid, gently rubbing my back and whispering soft words to me. The tears finally stopped, and I stayed where I was a few moments longer. Eventually, I untangled myself from him and crawled back into my own seat. Without saying anything, Kyle pulled open the glove box and handed me some shop towels before reaching over me to grab the seat belt and buckle me in. As he leaned back, I put a hand to his scruffy cheek and kissed his lips softly.

He sat back in his seat and put the truck into motion. Once we were on the road headed towards home, he reached over and took one of my hands in his. I looked at them on the console and smiled slightly. My rings sparkled in the sunlight coming through the windshield, and his work-worn, calloused hand gripped mine tightly.

Pulling into the driveway of what used to be his parent's farm, we bumped along with the potholes brought on by the winter frost. Kyle was planning on working on it this weekend, and I could see him flinch each time his truck hit a little too hard. When the old farmhouse came into view, I let out a breath. Bringing the truck to a stop in front of the house Kyle reached over again, this time to unbuckle the belt and to plant a kiss on my nose.

"Why don't you go in and take a warm bath and a nap. I am going to go tinker on that tractor some more to see if I can get it going without having to call JJ."

I nodded, kissing him briefly on the lips and jumping out. Trudging up the steps, I heard him put the truck in reverse and back across the yard to the large garage that housed our vehicles as well as a couple of pieces of farm equipment that we still had. I opened the screen door and heard the tell-tale slap of it against the frame as I closed the

Finding the Way Back
Marcie Shumway

heavy inside door behind me. I took the stairs two at a time and went directly into our master bath. Turning the knobs on the faucet connected to the claw tub, I set the temperature hot enough that it was barely tolerable and poured in some lavender bath soap.

As it filled, I shut the bathroom door and reached over to flick on the radio that was on the vanity. Meditation music filled the room, a mix of guitar and soft drumming. Undressing, I turned off the water as it reached a level that would cover me completely and I tested it with a toe. It was perfect, and the smell of the soap already worked to calm my frayed nerves.

No sooner was I submerged when the tears started once again. My poor husband thought he knew exactly what the problem with me was, however, I had been keeping a secret from him for almost a year, and he didn't have a clue. I didn't know how much longer I could keep it from him. My heart and mind were so heavy, and now that JJ and Skye had welcomed little Eric into the world, I felt like I was being slapped in the face. How could I tell him that I had lost our baby?

Chapter 2

Kyle didn't come back to the house until late that night. I had made and eaten supper alone, which was a normal occurrence when he was home lately. Once everything was put away, I had crawled into bed and immediately fallen asleep. I had been vaguely aware of him coming in and settling beside me. As always, we turned our backs to each other and slept. No touching, cuddling, or sex. The same as it had been off and on for almost a year.

I don't know what had happened to our marriage or when it had transpired, but I knew what had changed within me. Maybe that was what had caused everything else to take a steady downward spiral. There were times, like the day before, when things were fine, and we supported each other. Then there were times when it felt like we were nothing more than roommates or good friends. I despised that feeling.

Climbing out of bed the next morning, I found that I was once again alone. By the sounds, Kyle was still tinkering on the tractor, as I could hear it trying to turn over and then stopping. It seemed he would be calling JJ sooner rather than later. I made my way to the bathroom and stopped short when I reached the mirror. My shoulder length brown hair was a mess considering I had fallen asleep with it in a ponytail, but what really caught my attention was my blue eyes. Puffy from the crying the day before, they were sad and heartbreaking to look into. I ran my hand down my face and looked at my body. I wasn't nearly as thin as my best friends Skye Hunter and Lisa Brown, I had always had curves. However, I usually felt pride in those curves because I saw the way my husband looked at me, with lust and love. Today, I felt 100 lbs heavier than I truly was.

Taking a long hot shower, I didn't rush to get downstairs. I was hungry and more than ready for breakfast, yet I knew Kyle had already taken care of the animals, so I didn't need to rush for them. When I finally came down, I saw Kyle out the window. He was down to a long-sleeved t-shirt and his Carhartt jeans. Preparing the griddle to make French toast and starting the coffee pot, I admired the muscles that moved on his body. Whether it was his butt and thighs flexing as he squatted down or bent over, his forearms bunching and relaxing as he turned the wrench, or his should blades pressing against his shirt as he reached for something, the man still turned every part of me to goo.

I was just finishing up with the bacon and the last of the French toast when Kyle finally came in. He dropped a kiss on my head before moving to the sink to wash up. I put the food and condiments on the table while he made us cups of coffee. Bringing them over, he gently pushed me into the chair and pulled the orange juice from the refrigerator. We ate in companionable silence for a bit before he spoke up.

"I can't seem to get that thing going," he told me as he took a bite of bacon. "I think I am going to call Chad and see if he can help. I don't really want to bother JJ right now if I can help it, but we need that machine."

Chad Conrad had been our friend since high school, and he was currently engaged to one of my best friends, Lisa. His parents owned Conrad's Cabins & Lodge, a favorite getaway for many out-of-staters. JJ Hunter was married to my other best friend, Skye, and the two had just welcomed their first baby, Eric, into the world. JJ also happened to own a small engine repair shop.

"I completely understand," I agreed. "Do you want me to take the steer over to the Paterson's?"

We had about 25 head of beef cattle that we sold for meat, or pets if that's what people wanted them for. I was the one that cared for them for the most part due to Kyle's job. We also hayed our fields and sold what we didn't use to local horse and goat people that needed it.

"If you don't mind, that would be great," he answered. "I'll load them up for you when I go back out."

I didn't argue with him about the fact that I could easily hook up the truck and trailer, as well as load the calves. I had done it a hundred times. I knew he was trying to be nice after everything yesterday. When we were done eating, we went our separate ways, but not before he kissed me sweetly. My heart physically ached as he walked out the door and I cleaned up the kitchen.

Kyle thought he knew what had gotten me all upset yesterday. He assumed it was because we hadn't conceived yet. We had been trying for almost two years and each month my period had come. What he didn't know was that in February of last year we had gotten pregnant. I had been two weeks late before I had taken the test that had come out positive and he had been gone on one of his three-week rotations. I had waited until I had confirmation from the doctor before I told him. Unfortunately, when I finally got in I was already ten weeks, and he had been gone again. Two weeks later I had woken up in the middle of the night in a pool of blood and severe cramping. I had known almost immediately what had happened.

Putting on my boots, my jacket, and grabbing my gloves by the door, I headed outside. I still felt guilty for not telling him. He deserved to know. I was struggling with the loss myself, so I battled with coming clean with him. It was my fault that our baby was gone. Obviously, I had done something wrong. I was scared that he would be angry, after all, I had let him down. He deserved a woman that could give him the family he so badly wanted.

I reached the truck just as he was shutting and latching the back door of the trailer. I threw my gloves in the cab and did a quick check of the hook-up. I was aware that Kyle knew what he was doing. I was just a little OCD that way, double checking and triple checking things that I knew were in capable hands. When I was done, I turned and found him leaning against the door of the truck with a smirk on his face. The same smile that always made my heart skip a beat. I walked up to him and smacked him lightly before climbing in and allowing him to shut the door.

"You have the address, right?" he asked leaning in the open window as I buckled up and blasted the heater.

"Yep, I went with you when we brought the last two," I reminded him.

"So you did," he smirked again.

I kissed him quickly on the lips and pushed him to get him out of the window. He laughed as he stepped back and I shut it. Pulling away from him, I looked in the rearview and found him watching me. The smile he had had on his face was gone, replacing it was a thoughtful, sad look. I turned my attention back to the driveway and took a deep breath. I had the next two and half hours to myself to relax. It was an hour drive to the farm I was going to, and I knew I would be there at least a half hour between unloading and chatting.

When I had been on the road awhile, my thoughts strayed to my friends. Lisa had often taken these trips with me when Kyle had been gone for work. It was a great chance for us to catch up and vent. Skye and I had done a few runs in high school for Kyle's parents, but we hadn't seen much of each other since she had been home. I had kept my distance from both of them lately. I didn't know how to act when a piece of me was missing. They were both so happy in their relationships and Skye with a new baby, Eric.

As I slowed down to turn off the main road and head down the last long stretch before the Paterson's, my cell phone vibrated. I glanced at where it sat in the cup holder and saw that it was a message from Lisa. Speak of the devil. I ignored it and kept driving. It vibrated again, and when I glanced at it I had to fight back the tears, it was Kyle this time, and the message that lit my screen simply said *<3 U.*

It might finally be time to talk to someone. I couldn't keep this to myself much longer. I missed my friends. I missed my husband and my marriage. I missed *me.* The old me. The happy-go-lucky girl that everyone loved to be around and depended on. I didn't like the hermit I was becoming. As soon as Kyle went back to work, I would call my doctor. Yeah, as soon as he was gone.

<u>Chapter 3</u>

Sighing, I laid in bed watching my husband pack his bags to leave the following morning. Kyle worked on a hopper dredge boat whose company was based out of Seattle, but luckily it worked predominately on the east coast. A friend of the family had recommended the job when Kyle had finished his degree at the maritime college, and it had been the perfect fit.

The *George Stewart* had quickly become his home away from home. His hard work ethic had earned him high praise from others on the boat, and his infectious carefree attitude had earned him countless friendships. While I was happy he had found a job that he was passionate about and the money was enough to let us live comfortably, the three weeks on/off rotation had gotten old quickly. I missed having him home especially with our marital problems.

"What's going on in that pretty little head of yours?" Kyle asked as he put the bag he had just finished with by the door.

"That we need to find you a different job, one closer to home," I mumbled curling up on my side.

"If that's what you really wanted," he informed me, bending over to drop a kiss on my nose, "you know I'd do it in a heartbeat."

As he climbed back off the bed and headed to the bathroom, I pondered his comment. It was true. I knew he'd change what he was doing if I asked him to. However, I couldn't take him away from something he enjoyed doing. It would just give him another reason to resent me. I at least took comfort in the fact that he struggled with the distance as much as I did.

When Kyle came back out, my mouth watered and my body hummed at the sight of him. We had been high school sweethearts, married young, and made it through four years of college. Our eight years together had done nothing to squelch the desire that rose up each time I saw him in those boxer briefs that hugged him like a second skin.

It was obvious he was feeling the same. Before he leaned down to pull the blankets back and join me, I could see the bulge straining against the cotton. My arms came up on their own accord to pull him close and my legs wrapped around his waist as he settled himself over me. This was the part of our relationship that I never questioned, the time that my mind was most at peace, and I felt the closest to my husband.

His lips blazed a trail down my neck and across my collarbone as I ran my nails lightly over his muscles. Kyle made quick work of pulling his shirt I was wearing over my head. As soon as it was removed his mouth was hot and insistent on my left nipple. Electricity shot through me and I arched up against him, even thru the cotton I could feel the heat of his core against me.

"Too many clothes," I panted as he switched sides of my chest and I pushed at his boxers with my heels.

I heard his faint chuckle as he slid down my body, pulling my underwear down along the way. Gasping as his warm breathed teased over my throbbing clit, I looked down to admire him as he pulled off his boxer briefs. The lamp on the bedside table flickered shadows over the contours of his solid chest and stomach along with the light dusting of hair. His brown eyes were dark with desire and trained on me while he rubbed his lips and his five o'clock shadow up my body.

I gripped his buzzed dirty blonde hair and hauled his mouth back to mine. Our tongues dueled, and I shifted my pelvis to take him in. One quick thrust and he was sheathed to the hilt. I let out a long groan as he pulled out slowly and slammed into me again.

Kyle's movements were quick and his mouth nonstop, almost as though he knew what I needed. It wasn't long before we both climaxed. He slowly rolled off me and used his arm to bring me with him so that I was laying on his chest. Placing a kiss on his pec, I closed my eyes and let the steady beat of his heart lull me to sleep.

The next morning I was startled awake. My eyes sprang open, and I gawked around me trying to figure out why I felt so out of sorts. Looking at the clock, I realized why. It was eight o'clock, and I should have been up hours ago for chores and to see Kyle off. Instead, I was still in bed and naked at that. I sat up quickly and moved to jump out from under the covers when I realized I was alone and there was a note on my husband's pillow.

He had left a scrap piece of paper saying that he knew I needed the sleep, so he had taken care of the animals and had our friend Chad bring him to the airport. He finished off by telling me how much he loved me and that we would get through this together. Sighing, I flopped back down and snuggled back into the warmth. Guilt started to flood back in, bringing tears to my eyes. He deserved to know about the baby, yet I was so scared he was going to hate me for what I had done.

I'm not sure how long I dozed off for, but I was woken up by my cell phone. Ignoring it, I rolled over once again and when I checked the time I figured I should probably get up. I crawled out and made my way to the bathroom, my stomach growling along the way. After a quick shower, I dressed in worn jeans, a t-shirt, and a sweatshirt. I braided my hair as I went back to grab my phone from the top of the headboard where it was plugged in. I had two missed calls and four text messages.

I swiped my finger across the screen after I had secured my hair tie. The messages were all from Lisa and Skye. Rather than read or listen to them, I clicked the button to darken my screen once again and made my way downstairs for breakfast, or lunch depending on what you wanted to call it at this point.

It was no wonder I had fallen back to sleep, clouds covered the spring sky. The weather fit perfectly with my mood. I turned on the kitchen light, despite the time of day, and worked on making myself a grilled cheese sandwich and a veggie omelet. When my food was ready, I took it into the living room along with a glass of water and turned on the television.

While I ate, I pulled my phone back out and swiped across the screen. I thought a moment, chewing and listening to the hum of a soap opera on the TV. I wanted to send them each a message that would keep them from worrying any further and would also keep them from coming over to check on me in person. After a few moments, I settled on telling them that Kyle had just left, and we had a lot going on around the farm so I wouldn't be able to get together right away, but that everything was fine.

It didn't take long for the girls to respond and I let out a sigh of relief when I read the messages. Lisa told me that she and Chad were available if I needed anything, along with sending her love. Skye's wasn't much different, stating that JJ could help if need be and that she couldn't wait for me to spend time with her and little Eric. Tears filled my eyes and guilt filled me once again, only this time it was a different kind.

The past year had been tough on me, and somehow these amazing women had still stuck with me. They had taken my excuses in stride, always including me and repeatedly asking me if I needed anything. More often than not, they would show up at my doorstep with food, alcohol, and a movie, ready to cheer me up even though they didn't know exactly what was bothering me. How had I gotten so lucky? They didn't deserve the way I was treating them, and I didn't deserve their devotion.

Chapter 4

Waiting. I swear that was the worst part of trying to get pregnant. The two weeks of waiting after your missed period before taking a test are the longest two weeks ever. The little plastic stick that could change your life forever or break your heart. The fact that my cycle was so regular, even without birth control, meant that my patience was crucial to a positive test. Oh, and to those that tell you not to stress during that time, I am ready to tell them where they can put their advice.

I was a week late, and Kyle was due home the following week. I just wanted to know. I wanted to be able to tell him either way when he stepped through the door. I didn't mention anything to him over the phone about it. I figured I would tell him everything when he returned. If there was anything to share that is.

Trying to keep myself busy wasn't easy either. This time of year the animals only needed to be taken care of in the morning and at night which left the middle part of the day wide open. Spring weather is so unpredictable that it was hard to enjoy much time outside and a woman could only clean so much. At this point, I was pretty sure Kyle and I could eat directly off the floors without worrying about anything.

I toyed with the idea of reaching out to Lisa and Skye. However, I still wasn't sure if I was ready to share what was going on. I knew that they would support me, that wasn't even a question, yet how could I tell them if I couldn't even tell my husband?

Plus, the two of them were very busy with things in their own lives. Skye and JJ had just welcomed baby Eric, so they were settling into being new parents as well as being newlyweds. I couldn't have been happier for them. The fact that they had reunited after so many years apart was a sign they were truly meant to be. Lisa was planning her wedding to Chad as well as settling into their new house. That was a couple I never saw coming. Sure, he had always been there for her. However, I guess I had never noticed that he had fallen in love with her somewhere along the line.

Looking out the window, I decided that I needed out of the house. The spring sky was cloudless as I made my way down the porch steps and out to the barn. I pulled my jacket a little tighter around me after opening the doors and stepping inside. My eyes took a moment to adjust, but I didn't need them to. I knew the building by heart. The front half had been converted to box stalls and a tack room for the few horses we owned. We currently owned four, two of which would spend part of the spring, summer, and fall at Chad's parent's lodge doing trail rides with the guests.

Once I had all Mac's gear out, I made my way outside to the pasture to bring him in. I felt myself slowly relax as I set about the routine of brushing the dirt from his chestnut coat and tacking him up. He bumped me with his nose when I double checked the cinch on his girth, causing me to chuckle. Mac was a favorite at Conrad's for his steadfastness and ability to adjust to any rider.

When he was ready to go, I led him from the barn to our riding arena. Kyle had decided that in order for me to be able to ride year-round I needed a large riding ring. While it wasn't covered, the sand footing allowed me to ride no matter what time of year it was. We also chain dragged it with the tractor weekly.

Finding the Way Back
Marcie Shumway

I clipped on my helmet and led the gelding to the mounting block. He was more than ready to go and no sooner did my butt hit the saddle that he was moving. I chided him for moving without being asked, yet I couldn't put my whole heart in it considering I was just as happy to be on him. The steady swaying beat of his walk instantly calmed me.

I had left blue sand barrels strategically placed throughout the arena earlier on in the week, so Mac and I spent an hour first walking and then trotting patterns around them. After I gave him a loose rein, and with a slight touch of my heels, we were cantering around the outside rail of the arena. A few laps later, I sat down deep and allowed only my weight to slow him back down. He responded immediately, and when we were back at a walk, I leaned down and scratched his neck affectionately.

We walked a few more laps to make sure he was cooled down and headed back to the barn. I untacked him and gave him a quick brush down before letting him back out to join his friends. Once I put the saddle, bridle, and brush box back in the tack room I sat down on the bench outside the barn door. It had felt so good to not think for a little while.

Looking around, I smiled. Kyle and I had been very lucky in acquiring the farm. It had originally been owned by Kyle's grandparents, and when they had both passed away, everything had been left to his mother. Her and his father had worked the land as dairy farmers for years, much like the generation before them. When the economy had started to falter, they had decided that they needed to get out before they lost their retirement. My in-laws had kept some beef cattle around, mostly Herefords, for years after.

Signing the farm and the land over to Kyle and me

Finding the Way Back
Marcie Shumway

when we had finished college had been an easy decision for them. They were ready to retire and enjoy life without the huge responsibility. Florida had been calling their names. We saw them a couple of times a year when possible. The herd they had left us originally was mostly gone, but we kept a few from each line to keep breeding.

I closed my eyes and laid my head back against the wood. The light breeze tickled my nose with the smells of the animals and spring. Noises from the cows reached my ears, and I laughed when I heard a bleat that signaled one of the younger ones was running around. I was lucky to have this life. Even if pregnancy never came, I was blessed to have the things that I did.

Somehow, I made it to the night before Kyle was due home without going completely bonkers. I had had some cramping, but I still hadn't started my period. I was on edge. Deciding that I would take a test first thing the next morning, I climbed into bed early and attempted to read myself to sleep. Despite being so stressed, or maybe because of it, I was out in a matter of minutes.

"No!" I cried waking up just before the sun rose.

I ran into the bathroom, and the minute I started to pull down my underwear I knew. Old Aunt Flo had made her appearance. Cramps gripped my uterus, and sharp pains dug into my lower back. Taking care of business, I cleaned up and crawled back into bed. Tears flowed freely.

Hours later I dragged myself out of bed and got dressed. Unfortunately, Kyle wasn't home to cover chores this time. Dressing in a couple of layers since it was still chilly, I made my way to the barn and took care of the animals. I did the bare minimum figuring I would clean them out that evening when I would, hopefully, be feeling a little bit better.

When I got back inside, I made myself a cup of hot chocolate and scrambled eggs. The warm food helped my belly and gave me a little bit of energy. I dragged myself upstairs and changed into comfy leggings and a long sweater with wool socks. Grabbing my rice pack, I went back down to the kitchen to warm it up and then to the living room to curl up on the couch.

I remained there until lunch, only getting up for bathroom breaks and to warm up my pack. After making myself some soup and downing a couple of pain pills, the cramps finally seemed to be subsiding some. I was just finishing a movie when I heard the crunch of tires on the driveway.

Sitting up, I looked out the window and found Chad's truck in our yard. He had texted me that morning to let me know he would pick Kyle up at the airport. I got up and dashed through the kitchen to get out to the porch to meet my husband. The minute he grabbed his bag from the backseat and said good-bye to our friend, the tears started to well up in my eyes. Chad gave me a quick wave and turned his vehicle around to leave while Kyle made his way up the stairs.

"I'm so sorry!" I sobbed uncontrollably, launching myself into his arms the moment he got to the landing.

Chapter 5

"Good morning, ladies" I heard Kyle greet.

It was fairly warm for April, and I had opened a few windows around the house to let things air out. I hadn't heard a car pull up, but I was baking cookies with the radio cranked up, and I might have missed it while I was banging things around. Looking out the window I froze, Skye and Lisa stood talking to my husband with baby Eric in a carrier between them.

"She's inside baking," he told them. "Go on in."

I started to panic. I wasn't ready to face them. Putting my hands on the counter to stabilize myself, I took a couple of deep breaths. I could do this. These were women that I had known most of my life. They were my best friends. My timer went off just as the two of them came through the kitchen door.

Waving to them, I motioned for them to sit down while I grabbed my pot holder and pulled the last batch of chocolate chip cookies from the oven. Both ladies made themselves comfortable at the table, so once I had the cookies cooling, I grabbed my teapot to fill it and start warming water. Lisa, knowing what I was doing, got up and pulled mugs from the cupboard. She also grabbed tea bags from the canister on the counter.

This routine was one that was familiar and helped calm my nerves. The three of us had gotten together and had tea or coffee more times than I could count between our senior year of high school and Skye returning home to Maine. We all knew what the others liked and were at home in each other's kitchens.

Skye got up and took a plate from the drying rack by the sink and quickly filled it with cookies. I snuck a peak of Eric over my shoulder and noticed he was still sleeping soundly in his carrier, despite Skye having loosened his straps and uncovering him. When my teapot was just about to whistle, I pulled it from the stove and filled all three mugs. We met back at the table and settled in with our drinks and sweets.

"How's life as a new momma going?" I asked Skye as I toyed with my tea bag.

"Not bad," she said nibbling on a cookie. "Eric is a quiet baby. He sleeps all the time and barely fusses."

"I sense a but in there," I said looking up at her. Her voice was off, and she had a look on her face that I couldn't quite read.

"It's nothing," she said, waving it off. "How is engaged life, Lisa?"

While the conversation changed to Lisa and the things going on with her life, I eyed Skye. She looked a little tired, which was to be expected given she was a new mom, but there was something else there. Even though I had known her most of my life, I couldn't put my finger on it. I turned back to Lisa who was now telling us that she and Chad had set a date, so it was time to start doing some planning.

"I was wondering," she said nervously, reaching down into her purse and pulling out two shooter bottles of wine. "If you ladies would be my bridesmaids?"

Each bottle was marked with a label and a sweet message with her request. Despite everything going on with myself and the fact that I had been avoiding them, she still wanted me there beside her. Tears filled my eyes, and I stumbled from my seat to engulf her in a bear hug. Skye quickly joined us. Our squealing and crying didn't last long as Eric started to fuss. Obviously, our noises had woken him up, and he wasn't happy about it.

Skye removed herself from our tangle of limbs and scooped him up murmuring softly to him. Lisa put her arm around my waist, and the two of us watched her. The love she had for him was evident in her eyes, and the kiss she planted on his tiny head had my heart in my throat. She brought him over to us when he quieted and all but shoved him into my chest.

Somehow, she knew I wouldn't take him on my own. I cradled him and couldn't keep myself from leaning down to inhale the scent that was all baby. Sighing, I took in every feature. He looked up at me with his momma's eyes and his daddy's nose and mouth. Eric watched me as I checked him out, never making a peep. The weight of him in my arms had brought feelings, I didn't want to deal with in front of them, coming to the surface.

"I'm not feeling well," I stammered handing the bundle back to Skye and moving to grab our cups from the table. "I think you ladies should go."

I could sense their confusion and hesitation. Putting the mugs in the sink, I turned back to the table and grabbed the plate of cookies and placed it on the counter with the others I still had cooling on racks. Neither of them had moved, staring at me with concern and uncertainty. My eyes filled and I scooted by them before they started to fall.

I nearly fell trying to make it up the stairs as my sight was starting to blur. I ran down the hallway, shutting our bedroom door behind me and then closing myself in our master bathroom. A sob escaped me and tears streamed down my face that I was useless to stop. The pain radiated through my entire body.

I'm not sure how long I sat there and cried. So many emotions were balled up inside me dying to come out. I was angry that I couldn't get pregnant, I was sad that I had lost our baby, I was annoyed that Skye couldn't seem to appreciate what she had, I was upset because I missed my friends. Every time I thought the tears were done, they would start up again.

"Oh, baby," Kyle murmured coming into our bathroom.

He picked me up from where I was curled on my side on the floor and cradled me in his arms. His comfort only brought on more sobs and made me cry harder. I was keeping something so important from him. I wrapped my arms around his neck and buried my face in the crook of it.

"We will get pregnant," he whispered rubbing my back. "Please don't give up on that."

"What happens if we don't?" I asked wiping my face against his shirt.

"Then it will just be us," he answered matter-of-factly. "Would that be so bad?"

I chuckled slightly. It wouldn't be that bad, but how did you make that emptiness go away? How did you make that dull ache disappear? How did you move forward feeling like there was something missing in your family?

"We can get through anything together, Sam," he assured me, pulling back so he could use one hand to wipe my face.

"I know we can," I responded. "Did the girls leave?"

"Yes," he said with a confused look. "They were worried about you. I take it you haven't talked to them about the fact that we are trying?"

"I...I can't," I stammered unsure how I could explain

30

it to him.

"I wish you could," he admitted. "I think it would help."

I wiggled to get out of his arms, but he held fast. I was mad. I had no right to be, he hadn't done anything wrong. He just didn't understand. I wasn't going to unload my problems on them when they had their own stuff going on. There was something wrong with me, and they didn't need that.

"Don't be mad," he pleaded gathering me close again. "It was just a suggestion. You don't have to tell them if you don't want to."

I sighed and snuggled back into his warmth and smell. He might be right, it might help. Just like it might help to tell him. I kissed his neck and closed my eyes. Soon, I would tell them all everything. Soon.

Chapter 6

KNOCK! KNOCK! KNOCK!

I sat up straight on the couch, where I had been napping, disoriented and hazy. The last thing I remembered was finishing up on some housework and laying down to "rest" my eyes. Scrambling up, I headed to the kitchen where the sound had come from. Skye and Lisa stood on the other side of the door looking back at me.

"We brought lunch," Skye informed me as I opened the door.

"And dessert," Lisa said following her in.

"Okay…" I stammered, still trying to clear my groggy head. "Wait! Where's Eric?"

"He's with his gram for a few hours," Skye replied rummaging around in the bags and pulling out to-go containers from our favorite local restaurant, The Pit. "I didn't think he needed to listen to our adult conversation."

"Adult conversation?" I questioned, trying to catch up with them as they dropped the food and drinks on my table.

"Yes," Lisa commented, nudging me towards a chair. "Something is obviously up with you, so we are staging an intervention of sorts."

Suddenly I was awake. The fog cleared and I started to panic. I wasn't ready to share this with them. They couldn't make me. They wouldn't understand.

"That's it," Skye's voice cut into my train of thought. "That look tells me there is something going on. Don't try to deny it."

Finding the Way Back
Marcie Shumway

"It's nothing you two need to worry your pretty little heads about," I snapped. "You and your perfect lives."

I slapped my hand over my mouth as soon as the words came out and tears sprang to my eyes. The two of them stared at me, eyes wide and mouths gaping open. I had always been the voice of reason of the three of us, the most laid back, the buffer, and the happy-go-lucky. Now I was taking out my pain and frustration on the two women that meant the most to me, women that were like sisters to me.

"Guess we need to fill you in," Lisa stated breaking the silence that ensued.

"I'm sorry," I stuttered. "I didn't mean..."

"It's okay," Skye assured me putting her hand over mine on the table.

I couldn't look at her. It wasn't okay. They hadn't deserved the snide comment I had made. I finally looked back up from where Skye's and my hands were still joined and saw nothing but love and warmth in both their eyes.

"Did JJ ever tell you or Kyle the reason behind my coming home?" Skye asked.

I shook my head. I still remembered the night Chad had told us all she was moving back to Maine. The six of us had been so close in high school that when she went away to college, it had felt like a piece of me was missing. My heart had almost burst with happiness when I had found out about her return.

"Steve had become physically abusive," she said quietly, speaking of her ex from New York. "I came home to get away and start over, only to have him follow me here."

My mouth dropped open. How had I missed all that? I knew how. I had been so caught up in my own problems that I had let her down. I should have been there for her.

Unfortunately, my miscarriage had been horribly timed with her coming home.

"What do you mean when you say he followed you here?" I whispered, not trusting my voice.

"He snuck into our house and attacked me. It was right after I had found out that I was pregnant with Eric."

Tears now fell freely down my face. Skye squeezed my hand that she still held and Lisa quickly leaned over to grip my other one. How could she not hate me? I hadn't been there. Lisa had obviously found out at some point, so I was the one left in the dark. I was a horrible friend.

"Don't you dare blame yourself for not being there!" Skye scolded turning my face towards hers. "I kept it from everyone when I first came home. JJ was the first to find out and then the Conrad's."

"I should have been there for you!" I exclaimed on the brink of sobbing.

"How could you have been when you didn't know?" she asked wiping my face with her free hand.

"Let's eat some lunch before we continue," Lisa recommended after I had cried myself out in Skye's arms.

I didn't know how I could keep anything down with the emotions churning through me, but I knew I needed something in my stomach. The girls had gotten me a bacon, chicken, ranch wrap with a chocolate milkshake, my favorite lunch. We ate in silence, each of us lost in our own thoughts.

When we were all done, Lisa grabbed us bottles of water while Skye and I cleaned up the empty containers. We all decided that we would wait for dessert and headed into the living room to finish our talk. Lisa and I made ourselves comfortable on the couch while Skye sat down in Kyle's recliner with her feet tucked under her.

"Do you know how Chad got the black eye and the stitches he sported at New Year's Eve?" Lisa questioned.

I thought back to that night and realized that I didn't actually know what had happened to him. When I had thought to ask, someone had changed the subject. After that, I had chalked it up to him getting it doing something at the lodge. Shaking my head, I moved so that I was facing her.

"He got it from my stepbrother, James. The man that had sexually abused me from the time I was ten until I was fourteen."

Again, tears flowed freely down my face. How could these two still want to be near me? She leaned over and wrapped her arm around my shoulders. Why the hell was she comforting me?

"You ladies should hate me. I'm never there for you when you need me!"

"Sam, you and Kyle weren't even around when everything happened. Everything came out at Christmas time while you two were in Florida," Lisa said moving her hand down to rub my back.

"How can you two comfort me?" I shrieked jumping up from my spot on the couch to pace the living room. "I haven't been here when you both needed me the most."

"You didn't know," Skye argued, sitting up a bit in her chair. "Neither of us shared our secrets until it was almost too late. We don't want that for you. That's why we are here."

I stopped moving and looked at her. That's when I saw it. The worry etched on both of their faces, the concern in their eyes. I sat down on the coffee table with a *thud* and motioned for Skye to come over and sit by Lisa in front of me. Once she did, I reached out to take one of each of their

35

hands in mine. It was time for me to tell them my story.

"First off, I am still going to struggle with not being there for you two when I should have been. I'm sorry that I was so wrapped up in my problem that I couldn't be. As best friends, we are supposed to stand by each other through thick and thin. Instead, I dug myself into a hole that I don't know how to get out of."

Both women started to speak, but I put my finger up to silence them. I wasn't done and knew that if they spoke, I would never get out what I needed to. Taking a deep breath, I looked down at our joined hands and started telling them what had happened.

"Kyle and I had been trying to get pregnant for a few months when I finally got a positive pregnancy test. I wanted to make sure the test was correct, so I didn't say anything to Kyle. I finally got in to see the doctor, and I was ten weeks along, but he had gone back out to work. Two weeks later I lost the baby."

Tears flowed yet again, this time they weren't mine. Lisa and Skye had streams running down their faces. I took a couple of deep breaths and worked on getting out the last little bit. The part that was eating me alive.

"I haven't told Kyle yet," I told them, my voice quiet. "I don't know how to tell him I screwed up. I am so scared he will resent me."

"He doesn't know?!" Lisa questioned.

"What do you mean you screwed up??" Skye asked.

"It's my fault that the baby is gone. Obviously, I did something wrong," I told her.

"Oh honey," she gripped my hand tighter between both of hers. "You didn't do a darn thing wrong. There had to have been something wrong with the baby. The body knows what to do."

Finding the Way Back
Marcie Shumway

The doctor had told me the same thing, but all I could think when Skye repeated it was that she said it to make me feel better. If that was the case, then how come I hadn't gotten pregnant again. I took care of myself, the doctor had cleared me, and I followed an app on my phone to a tee each month to know when I ovulated. In my head, that pointed to me being the problem.

"I've heard the more you stress about it, the less likely it is to happen," Lisa voiced bringing me back to our conversation. "I'm sure the strain of handling this alone doesn't help."

"I'm not alone now," I reminded her.

<u>Chapter 7</u>

"How about this one?" Lisa asked stepping in front of the mirror for what felt like the millionth time.

"If you have to ask then it's not the one," Skye informed her with a smile as she burped Eric on her shoulder.

Our friend stuck her tongue out at us and made her way back to the changing rooms with a *huff*. We couldn't help but laugh in her wake. We had decided on a whim to drive almost two hours south to Pigmont. The town was filled with small shopping centers and the largest mall in the state. Since Lisa didn't want a traditional wedding dress, we didn't need to hit the bridal stores which was a huge relief to us.

"Think she has "the one" in there?" I questioned taking a sip of my smoothie.

"Yep and it's probably the last dress she thought it would be."

We would be wearing sundresses, so I got up and wandered to some racks to see what I could find. Skye followed suit once Eric was content and handed him to me on her way by, clearly on a mission. I put him on my shoulder, bouncing lightly as I picked through dresses with my free hand. After telling the girls my secret, being around the baby had been getting easier.

"Oh!" Lisa's gasp had us both turning our heads.

She stood in front of the mirrors once again, but this time her hands covered her mouth and tears were filling her eyes. The two of us smiled at each other and made our way to her side. Eric was dozing, so I placed him back in his carrier before joining the girls in front of the largest mirror.

Lisa had opted to remain traditional in the color of the dress, so it was white, but that's where the similarities with a regular wedding dress ended. The top was a halter style and it fitted to her body with a slit flare where it ended just above her knees. Simple sequins lined the heart shaped top that covered her chest, the straps that went around her neck, and the fabric that wrapped around her back. It fit her perfectly.

"Wait!" Skye exclaimed turning to the other bags from our shopping trip.

She pulled out a pair of beautiful white cowboy boots that had hearts cut out near the top that were surrounded by almost the same sequins as the dress. They were a perfect match. Lisa started shaking her head, but Skye moved to help her put them on her feet.

"There," Skye said once they were on. "Perfect."

After a little half-hearted arguing, Lisa gave in on the boots. Skye and I had found them and knew they would be just what she needed for her special day. Once the tears were done being shed, Skye and I went back to looking at dresses for ourselves while Lisa changed out of hers.

"How about these?" I asked holding up matching style sundresses.

They both had thin double straps that crisscrossed in the back and fell just at the knee. We had decided on brown cowboy boots for us, and the soft pink and blue of the material would look awesome. She clapped her hands together like a child, and we giggled as we headed to the dressing rooms to change.

"Hurry up you two!" Lisa hollered at us.

I stepped out first and was stunned when I moved to

the mirror. The blue set off my eyes and made them seem larger than they actually were. Skye came out and stood beside me. The pink set off the glow she had seemed to acquire with motherhood. Lisa's eyes welled up again, and I knew we had found what we were looking for.

Finishing up our girls day, we packed everything into Lisa's Jeep and headed for The Pit. We were going to grab dinner there before heading home. By the time we pulled in, we were giggling like high schoolers and ready for a good meal and a round of drinks.

One of our regular waitresses saw us come in the door and directed us to our favorite booth. We settled in and had wedding talk while we waited. I lost track of time and the next thing I knew my meal was gone. Not only that, but I had downed multiple shots and two mixed drinks. My head was light, my words on the edge of slurring, and my emotions running high. Hence the reason I didn't normally drink like that.

"Okay, darling," Lisa said steering me out of the restaurant and to her SUV. "Let's get you home."

Somehow, between the two of us, I got buckled into the passenger side of her car. Skye opted for the back with Eric just in case the short drive made me sick. I knew it wouldn't come to that, I wasn't that far gone.

We pulled down my long driveway, and I started to feel weepy. I knew that Kyle was at home waiting for me and I felt the guilt rear its ugly head. I must have made a noise because Lisa looked over at me concerned. Waving her off, I pinched the bridge of my nose and let out a long breath.

Someone must have texted Kyle, he was waiting on the porch with the outside light on when we pulled to a stop. I climbed out on my own, but Lisa met me at the front of the car. She engulfed me in a hug, and I squeezed her back with all my might.

"Thank you so much for coming today and for being my bridesmaid," she whispered. "It means more to me than you know."

Tears pricked the back of my eyes, and I rolled them up to keep them from filling. Pulling away from her I made my way to the side of the car where Skye was standing with the door open so she could hear Eric. I hugged her as well. While I was pulling away and turning towards my husband, I heard the baby fuss. My stomach dropped, and my heart started to pound.

Kyle met me at the bottom of the stairs, and I launched myself into his arms. Streams of tears flowed down my cheeks. He whispered sweet nothings in my ear, and I felt him move his arm to wave the girls off. My legs started to buckle, and he easily picked me up and carried me into the house. I wrapped my arms around his neck and sobbed into it.

His smell and the warmth of his body had me melting. I had to tell him. I couldn't keep this up any longer. The alcohol was just the liquid courage I needed. Kyle kicked the front door closed with his foot and walked into the living room. He didn't put me down, just simply sat down on the couch holding me and rubbing my back.

"I'm….so……sorry," I hiccupped trying to control the flow of water that didn't seem to want to stop.

"You have nothing to apologize for, sweetheart" he assured me, a smile to his voice.

"Our baby!" I wailed, crying so hard I coughed, and dry heaved.

"Sam, you need to calm down," he told me, moving me from his lap and turning to face me, cupping my cheeks

41

in his hands so he could force me to look at him. "Breathe."

I tried to do as he said, but when I thought about how upset he was going to be it started all over. Finally, with a little coaching from my wonderful husband I calmed down enough to open my eyes. Confusion was etched on his face. I reached out my hand and stroked it down his stubbly cheek.

"Okay, that's better," he soothed. "Now, what do you mean, our baby?"

"I lost it," I whimpered, dropping my eyes.

"Samantha, are you saying that you were pregnant?"

"I was 12 weeks along," I informed him, bringing my eyes back to his when his fingers stilled on my face. "I messed up."

Chapter 8

I woke up the next morning disoriented with a pounding headache and a sour stomach. If that hadn't been enough to remind me of what had happened the night before, rolling over to a cold bed where my husband should have been, would have. Kyle had been the doting husband the night before, cuddling me until I calmed down, giving me a glass of water to ward off the coming hangover, and tucking me into bed. Looking over, I knew he had never joined me.

Slowly rolling to my side, I braced myself up and looked at the alarm clock, eight o'clock. Not bad, but I was sure Kyle already had the animals taken care of for the morning. My stomach seemed steady despite the sour feeling, so I made my way to the bathroom to take a hot shower. I needed to feel somewhat human again before I had to face my husband.

Making my way downstairs twenty minutes later in jeans and a t-shirt with a sweatshirt over my arm, I found the kitchen empty. Kyle's coffee mug sat in the sink, rinsed, but that was the only sign he had been there. I sighed and went to the stove to grab the kettle to take it to the sink to fill it. While it warmed, I put bread in the toaster and munched on a banana. I peeked out the window over the sink and saw no hint of my husband or his truck. I was uneasy. I didn't like not knowing what he was thinking or feeling.

I finished my breakfast and Kyle still wasn't back. Deciding that keeping busy was the best thing for me, I put on my sweatshirt, boots, and a light jacket and made my way outside. The animals had all been fed, but nothing had been cleaned yet, so I set to work. When I got to the horse pasture, I was greeted with knickers. I knew I shouldn't ride considering they would pick up on my unease, so I opted for grooming all of them instead.

At some point during my chores, I had faintly registered the sound of a truck. Despite the fact that he had come home, he had made no effort to come find me. Tears pricked my eyes as I closed the gate behind me and headed to the house. I heard him in the garage tinkering on something, but I kept going. The next move was his.

Lunch came and went, still no Kyle. I started getting fidgety. Finally deciding I needed to leave before I went crazy, I grabbed my purse and keys. Noise from the front porch had me freezing in the living room.

"Oh for god's sake," I muttered to myself. "When did I become afraid of my husband?"

"Probably about the same time you started talking to yourself," came the retort from the doorway.

My head snapped up and found him leaning on the wall with his arms across his broad chest. He was dressed just like I was with a baseball cap pulled low so I couldn't see his eyes. However, the tense muscles and the tick in his jaw told me what I needed to know. He was angry.

"You can't run from me," he stated moving forward, but not coming close enough to touch me.

"Why not? You've been doing it all day," I snapped.

He pulled off his hat and ran his hands through his short hair in frustration. I heard him let out a deep sigh that ended with a soft groan before he took my hand in his and tugged me towards the couch. He plucked my keys and my purse from my fingers and placed them on the coffee table.

Finding the Way Back
Marcie Shumway

"Obviously we need to talk," he stated holding my hands in his again, his eyes glued to mine.

"Yes," I muttered fighting to keep looking at him, to keep my scared gaze on his warm, caring one.

"Do I need to get you a shot?" he asked lightly, squeezing my hands.

"Definitely not," I replied with a soft smile. "I found out I was pregnant at the end of April, early May, last year."

His breath hitched as I told him the whole story. About not telling him until I was sure because I wanted to save us the heartbreak that we had been through so many times before, only to have it be way worse than a normal late testing, about keeping the miscarriage from him because I didn't want him to know about my failure as a mother or as a wife, and about the fact that I loved him more than I could ever express. When I stopped talking all that could be heard was my muffled sniffles and his labored breathing. He had gotten up to pace. However, he didn't say a word.

"You kept this bottled up for a year?!" he growled, tossing his hat on the recliner and running his hands roughly through his hair again.

"Yes, I was afraid you would be angry with me," I mumbled wiping the tears from my cheeks. "Which was obviously a good call."

"You think I'm mad because you lost the baby?!" Kyle questioned, finally coming to a stop across the room from me.

"It looks that way...." I started.

"I'm pissed you lost the baby, but I'm not upset with you. I'm angry at the universe for taking something we have wanted for so long. I'm also mad because you felt that you couldn't tell me," he told me sitting down beside me, yet not touching me. "Obviously, I'm not doing my job as a husband if you don't feel like you can come to me about something as important as that."

I was taken back. I had been so wrapped up in worrying about him being upset with me that I never thought about the fact that it was the first time I had ever kept anything from him in our almost seven-year marriage, heck in our entire life together. We had been best friends before we were a couple. He knew me better than anyone.

"Oh, my gosh, Kyle, no," I stammered trying to come up with the words I needed. "You haven't done anything wrong. I felt like it was all my fault and I didn't want you to resent me."

"You losing our baby was something beyond your control," he told me kissing the tears from my cheeks as some started to fill his eyes. "I could never resent you. You are my everything. You always have been."

Moving to straddle him, I captured any further words with my mouth on his. Without removing his lips from mine, he slipped his hands under my shirts and around my back to pull me down harder against his growing jean clad member. Letting out a purr against his mouth I pulled away quickly to shuck my clothes. No sooner had I finished stepping out of my underwear and pants did Kyle put his hands on my hips and pull me back down to straddle him.

He slid into me slowly, bringing his mouth back to mine to kiss me long and deep. One of my hands gripped his naked shoulder while the other wrapped around the back of his neck to grip his buzzed head hard. The pace and emotions were almost too much to bear causing streams to flow down my face as he lifted and lowered me slightly over and over.

Stretching out my legs, I slid them around him and

locked them against his lower back driving him even deeper. He groaned, and when I pressed my forehead against his to rock with him, I saw tear tracks on his face as well. Kyle shifted, driving his pelvis against my clit as he palmed one of my breasts gently in rhythm to our movements. That was all I needed, and my insides clamped around him taking him over with me.

As we sat there catching our breaths, I kissed his cheeks where the tears had left their trails. He rubbed his hands gently up and down my lower back giving me body little chills. I rested my forehead against his and looked into his sweet brown eyes. This man completed me.

"Don't ever do that again," he whispered. "We are in this together."

Chapter 9

       I stepped out onto the sidewalk, and my whole body shivered. It wasn't cold by any means. Actually, it was a warm spring day, and the sun felt good against my face and my arms bared by my t-shirt. Kyle came up beside me after holding the door open for a person coming into the old brick building as we were coming out. He reached over to thread our fingers together, giving me a gentle tug to head towards the truck. I squeezed his hand in return.

       We had taken the first step in moving past the miscarriage together, going to the doctors. I had seen my OBGYN the day after it had originally happened, yet I hadn't stepped foot back in her office or called her since. There had really been no need to, or so I had thought. Kyle had recommended we go back and see her to make sure everything was okay and that we didn't have anything to worry about.

       She had given us a clean bill of health based on what she had seen and said she would have the test results by the end of the week from the exam. My nerves were a mess leading up to the appointment, and my whole body would convulse every few minutes. It was draining, and I felt like I could easily curl up and take a nap for hours.

       "How are you holding up?" Kyle asked as he opened the truck door for me to climb inside.

       "Okay," I told him grabbing the handle inside and pulling myself up. "Ready to go home."

       "One more stop, baby," he reminded me, patting my leg before he shut the door and moved around the vehicle to get in himself.

I had agreed to see a counselor with him. I had seen one for years before, from childhood until I was finishing high school. My father had abandoned my mother and myself when I was young, so long ago I had no memory of him. Unfortunately, my mother had blamed me, leading us to have a very distant relationship. Duncan and Karen Conrad had taken me under their wings like they had with many others, and counseling had actually been their recommendation. I wasn't looking forward to it because I knew it would be emotionally difficult and would probably dredge up feelings of the past. However, I had agreed for him.

When my husband pulled the truck into the parking lot of a familiar white and gray farmhouse on the outskirts of town, I turned and looked at him with confusion. This was the same place where Mrs. Briggs had had her practice. He had made the appointment for us, and I hadn't questioned him figuring that he would find someone that would suit both our needs as a couple and individually. Kyle shut down the vehicle and kissed the back of my hand that was still held firmly in his.

"I thought you might be more comfortable returning to old stomping grounds," he told me, his cheeks coloring slightly. "I wanted you to be able to open up and thought this might be the best place to come."

I leaned over the center console and cupped his cheek with my free hand before moving in to kiss him softly on the lips. This man warmed my heart and soul in more ways than I could ever show him. His thoughts were always for me ahead of himself. I hadn't thought that who we saw really mattered until he pulled into this sanctuary and my body seemed to instantly relax.

Finding the Way Back
Marcie Shumway

"Thank you," I whispered stroking his face. "I can't tell you how much this means to me."

Shrugging his shoulders, he gave me another quick kiss and opened the door to jump out. I waited for him to come around and open my door for me, taking deep breaths in and out to steady my stomach. While the muscles in my body had let go, my internal organs were still playing pond hockey. I jumped out and instantly took hold of Kyle's arm when we started for the front porch.

No one from the outside would have ever known that this was a building filled with psychiatrists and counselors. It was an early 1900s farmhouse that had been converted into small offices, the barn had long ago come down. It sat on about 4 acres of gorgeously manicured greenery and was very welcoming. When you entered, you came into a parlor type room with a loveseat and a recliner. The room had a large window that looked out the side of the house into a small, well-taken-care-of garden. I knew the rest of the downstairs held the professional offices, a bathroom, and a small kitchenette. They had converted the five bedrooms upstairs into small meeting rooms of varying themes.

I took in the familiar smells of vanilla and clove as we walked in the door and the backs of my eyes stung. This place, other than the Conrad's lodge, had been my saving grace growing up. I wouldn't have become the adult I was without these ladies. Granted, I had been a client of Mrs. Briggs, the other women in the practice had always been available and caring if she hadn't been able to see me.

My husband directed us to the loveseat and we sat down hip-to-hip with his arm tucked tightly around my lower back. I laid my head on his shoulder and let out a deep sigh. He put his other hand on my thigh and gave it a gentle squeeze just as we heard footsteps coming down the hallway.

"Hello there," came a voice from my past.

I lifted my head and found the woman that had helped me through every crisis of the early part of my life. She hadn't seemed to have aged. Her blonde hair still hung in waves down her back, her blue eyes were filled with warmth, and her body was covered in a flowery flowy dress. The bracelets on her arms chimed lightly as she moved towards me while the flats on her feet barely made a sound.

I jumped up from the couch and was in her arms the instant she was close enough. She hugged me fully before setting me back to inspect me. A smile graced her lips, one that widened when she looked over and saw Kyle. The man was attractive, that I wouldn't argue, but his smile had always been something that could capture any woman without him even meaning to. Obviously, she was no exception.

"This gentleman must be Kyle," she stated, releasing me and turning to take one of his hands in hers. "You are the one that called."

"Yes ma'am," he answered, moving to place a hand on my back after he shook hers. "I thought maybe you could help us."

"Of course," she replied, waving for us to follow her back down the hall and up the wide staircase.

Meditation music floated around the upper level of the building. She opened a door at the end of the hall and ushered us in ahead of her. It was the green room, the one that had always been my favorite growing up. The walls were painted a mint green, and instead of furniture to sit on, there were pillows in several different shapes and sizes. I couldn't tell you what about it had drawn me in. Maybe it had been the fact that I could easily pretend that I was somewhere far away from my "real" life here and that nothing negative could get to me.

I knew this was a place that I could be me and there would be no judgment. I waited for Kyle to get comfortable and got a strange look from him when I hadn't moved from my spot by the door. Once he was settled, I sat between his legs and leaned my back against his chest. I needed the contact, and I needed his strength to get me thru this. From experience, I knew things were about to get emotional and raw. Kyle was my rock.

"So," Mrs. Briggs questioned, sitting with her legs crossed on a large pillow while her arms hung loosely down and her wrists rested on her knees, "what are we here to talk about today?"

"Our baby."

Chapter 10

"Maybe I should take some time off," Kyle commented as we sat at the kitchen table eating pancakes two weeks later.

"I'm fine," I assured him for the hundredth time that morning.

We had spent the past two weeks having therapy on Tuesdays and Thursdays knowing Kyle would eventually need to return to work. He was amazing and supportive, but space would do me some good. I was worn out emotionally and physically from everything. I was looking forward to a little time with my horses, and for reflection of the stuff we had dug up from my past.

"Are you positive?" he asked, leaning over to cup my cheek in one of his hands.

I nodded, smiling at him, and put my hand over his to squeeze before getting up to clear the table. Any conversation about my mother had always been taboo in our house. Yes, my husband knew about my past as we had been friends in school long before we ever became a couple, but it wasn't something I liked to talk about. I had blamed myself for my father leaving, just as she had until I had started seeing Mrs. Briggs regularly. Now, rehashing all of it depressed me.

Mrs. Briggs was a strong believer in the fact that things that happened in our childhood influenced our actions as an adult, whether it was good, bad, or indifferent. She felt that my sadness and anxiety about losing the baby had to do with my own fear of being a mother. After not carrying to term, I had been scared I would never be able to care for a child. I was also stressed that when we did have kids, I would be a detached mother much like my own.

It wasn't to say that I didn't want a child because I did in the worst way. Our little family was missing something. I think I had always had this subconscious worry that I wouldn't have good maternal instincts, despite everyone commenting throughout my life that I would be a good mother. When we had started writing down how we felt about the miscarriage, the fears had come to light.

Strong arms circled me from behind while I was lost in thought looking out the window and letting the warm soapy water fill the sink. I leaned into Kyle and the strength that he gave me. He pushed me without overdoing it, he held me without question, and he loved me without conditions. I had been damn lucky in finding a man like him at such an early age. There was no doubt in my head or my heart that we would make it through all this. It was just a matter of when.

"I don't like the idea of leaving you right after we have opened up all these old wounds," he murmured pulling me tighter against him and nuzzling into my neck.

"It will be good for me. I can work with the horses and get Mac and Lilly ready to head to Conrad's," I told him, rubbing my hands up and down his arms.

He kissed my cheek and released me to grab the remaining dishes and cups from the table. My husband had never had a problem leaving for his stints on the boat, at least not visibly. This time I could tell by the creases on his forehead and the worry in his eyes, he was. I didn't know how to put him at ease.

We finished cleaning up in silence. I could tell Kyle's brain was very busy, so I let him be. While I ran upstairs to shower and change my clothes, he took his bag out to the truck and started it. This time I would be taking him to the airport, rather than Chad.

Twenty minutes later we were stopping at Doc's Donuts outside of town for coffee. It was an hour and a half drive one way, and it was fairly early, but I would definitely need the caffeine to deal with interstate traffic on the way home. It also helped considering the first part of the ride was quiet, not uncomfortably so, just each lost in our own thoughts. I nearly jumped out of my seat when he finally spoke.

"I agree with Mrs. Briggs," he started, shifting slightly to grip my hand tighter on the center console.

"Oh?" I questioned, turning slightly to face him. "About what?"

"I think that you should talk to the girls again. Get yourself out and doing things with them," he said. "You've always been close to Lisa and Skye, and in the past year you have really pulled away."

"I know," I sighed. "I didn't want to burden them when they both had so much already going on. More than I even realized."

"They might have," he agreed, "but those girls love you like a sister and have never turned their backs on you."

"True."

"I am here for you, I'm not saying that I'm not," he said turning on the blinker for the off-ramp. "However, there are ways they can be there for you that I can't."

I squeezed his hand and turned my attention out the window to the passing scenery of the city. I knew he was right. There was something to be said for the sisterhood between girlfriends. They always seemed to understand even if they truly didn't, and they would fight as fiercely for you as your blood relatives. Here I was again, worrying about putting my crap on them and crying on their shoulders. The two of them had never given me a reason to feel this way. It was just me not wanting to saddle them with my problems. Meanwhile, I would take theirs on in a heartbeat.

"I'll think about it," I caved.

He nodded his approval, and I saw some of the earlier stress leave his face. Knowing I had the rest of our crew when he was away made him feel that much better about it. He navigated the vehicle through the complex roads and parking lots leading up to the front of the airport. It was just nearing 8 o'clock on a Wednesday morning, and the place was filling quickly. Pulling up to the curb, he threw it in park, and we both jumped out.

"I love you more than anything in this world, Samantha," he whispered when we met at the front of the truck, his hands cupping my face.

"I love you too," I whispered back, tears filling my eyes.

I wasn't normally emotional when it came to the drop offs, but with everything going on I couldn't contain them, and they spilled over onto my cheeks. Kyle wiped them away with his thumbs and kissed the tracks before brushing his lips across mine in a tender kiss that had my knees buckling. We parted, and he reached back into the truck to grab his bag. Throwing it over his shoulder, he walked towards the entrance. I was just about to climb in to drive away when I saw that he had stopped and was watching me. A small smile graced his face, and he blew me a kiss before turning back to head in the sliding glass doors.

That kiss kept a smile on my face the entire ride home. Even the internal battle I waged about whether or

Finding the Way Back
Marcie Shumway

not to call Lisa or Skye didn't remove it. I took a deep breath and figured I would just let my brain take me where I needed to go. The next thing I knew I was pulling back into town and Doc's Donuts. I ordered drinks for all three of us and drove to Hunter's Rig Repair. It would be easier to grab Lisa first and go to Skye since she had Eric.

I put the truck in park in front of the shop and was happy to see Lisa's Jeep in the driveway. Leaving it running, I hopped out and went straight in and to her office, bypassing JJ who was at the front counter talking to a customer. When I got to her doorway, I picked up the lightweight jacket from the chair at her conference table and motioned for her to follow me. She didn't question me, just got up and grabbed her cell phone.

The ride to the Conrad's was quick. I parked in front of the lodge, and the two of us gathered the drinks and donuts before going in. We found Skye in her office, right where I knew she would be. Despite the baby things strewed about, I saw no sign of Eric and figured he was with Karen or Duncan somewhere. She looked up with surprise when we walked in.

"Hey ladies," she greeted, turning her computer chair towards us. "To what do I owe this visit?"

"You'll have to ask her," Lisa told her nodding towards me and pulling the drinks from the travel tray.

"We are overdue for some girl time," I said, settling down into Karen's office chair as they both looked at me, "and, along with Kyle, I need you two to get through this."

57

Chapter 11

"You know you're going to have to get over that grumpiness," I murmured to Lily as I tightened her girth, "otherwise, Chad isn't going to let you play with the kids."

The mare threw her head, which to me was the equivalent of a teenager rolling their eyes. I patted her on the neck and led her over to the mounting block. Making sure my helmet was secure, I put my foot in the stirrup and mounted in one fluid motion. Or at least I thought I did, the next thing I knew I was sitting on the ground and Lily's dapple gray butt was dancing away from me with her dark tail flagging in the breeze.

"Hmph," I grunted getting up and dusting off my pants. "Clearly someone is feeling her oats this morning."

I tried two more times and had the same results. I wasn't hurt, but my pride was sure stinging. I heard a chuckle from the direction of the gate, and I found my cousin Rick leaning on it, shaking his head with a grin a mile wide on his face. I couldn't help it, and despite my frustration with the little mare, I laughed. Dusting myself off once again, I ambled over to where he stood and leaned against the galvanized metal while I watched Lily prance around like she had won the Kentucky Derby.

"Looks like you are letting that little thing get the better of you today," he commented, not bothering to hide his mirth at my dismay.

"You know how she is in the spring," I told him as I waited for her to come back to me, which she always did. "Once we get a couple rides in she will be all set to go.

Funny how she never does this with the kids."

"You're her momma and, just like the two-legged variety, they know they can get away with stupid stuff with you," he said, laughing again when she came up and pushed her head against my chest.

"Is that how it really is?" I asked with a sigh.

"Yep and you'll find it out soon enough."

"I'm not so sure about that," I whispered as I pulled the girth tighter once again.

"It will happen for you two when it's meant to," Rick theorized, "and when it does, you will find that it isn't all that different from how you are with these guys. You will be a wonderful mom."

"Even with what I came from?" I questioned, my heart in my throat.

Rick knew better than anyone what I was referring to. He was actually my second cousin and had been raised alongside my mother when his parents had died in a horrific car crash. When my mother had started to distance herself from me, he and his wife, Louisa, had gladly taken me under their wings along with Karen and Duncan Conrad. Both of their sons were older than I was and had moved out of state at the first opportunity, so they often joked that I was the only child they had left to dote on.

We had even hired on Rick to help us when we needed an extra hand on the farm. He owned his own landscaping company, Pride Property Maintenance, and had a solid crew that he could trust to handle things when he wasn't around. Louisa loved that he had some flexibility and that he could help us when we needed it. She worked for the Conrad's at the lodge cleaning and cooking. The regular families that visited adored her and knew her by name the same way they did the family that owned it. They were the parents I never had.

"Despite it," he assured me. "You have a warm and gentle heart. You're mother never had that. She wasn't meant to have children."

"Well, we have that in common," I grumbled.

Rick gave me a look that was both confusion and sadness. Playing with the reins I still held, I told him about the miscarriage and our battle. He was family, and I figured if I could open up to anyone it would be him. While I talked, I noticed that somewhere along the lines he had aged. Grey teased his temples and was mixed in with the dark hair on his head and his beard. Years of working outside had given him crow's feet and a semi-permanent tan, but there were more wrinkles and lines than I remembered. His wise, kind eyes remained on me the entire time I talked, but he did move to the gate to stand beside me. When his arm came up and around my shoulders, I leaned into him and sighed at the familiar comfort.

"I'll tell you this as many times as it takes to get it through that thick skull of yours," Rick started, holding me tightly against him. "You have a warm, gentle heart and you will be an amazing mother when the time is right. I know it is easier said than done but just relax. Work through what you need to with your husband and enjoy the time you two have together."

I squeezed him for all I was worth and stepped back. Even though I had heard those words from a million other people, hearing them from him made it better. Never in my life had Rick let me down, not even in the smallest way. I felt as though a huge weight had been lifted and like the final piece to the puzzle had been set in place.

Wiping away my tears, I led Lily back to the mounting block with newly found determination. My cousin followed to hold her head while I swung on. When I settled on her back and gathered my reins, he patted my leg a couple of times and stepped to the side taking the block with him, so it wasn't in my way. I walked her out to the rail and let my body move with her smooth, quick gait.

I couldn't agree more with Winston Churchill when he said: *"Something about the outside of a horse is good for the inside of a man."* Anytime I was on the back of one of my horses, my mind would clear, and my body would relax. It was the best kind of drug.

Putting her through a warm up doing circles and stretching, I could tell she was already itching to pick up the pace. For the next hour, we walked, trotted, and cantered different patterns from figure eights to serpentines to barrels and everything in between. Lily did everything I asked and never faltered, remaining true to the lesson horse I knew her to be.

As I cooled her down, I noticed that Rick still stood at the gate watching me. I smiled at him, and he returned it. I could remember riding at the Conrad's as a teenager and having him watching me as I took lessons from Karen. I had never been one for extracurricular activities at school, yet I had taken to horseback riding like a fish to water. Even then it had been my means of escaping the reality that was my life. My cousin had admitted that he had always enjoyed watching me, that there had been something on my face when I sat on a horse that nothing could compare to.

"I'm going to head out, kid," he told me when I brought Lily over to him so I could dismount. "I have a job to check out in Oak Cove."

"Okay. Thank you so much for coming over," I replied leaning to hug him and give him a kiss on his weathered cheek.

Finding the Way Back
Marcie Shumway

"Just wanted to check on you and the stock," he scoffed. "No big deal. I'll be back next week when Deke comes to do the inoculations."

"Good," I laughed, "I wasn't looking forward to holding those buggers on my own. They are getting too big."

He chuckled at my comment and turned to head back to the driveway where his truck was parked. His hand came up in one last wave, and I blew him a kiss like I had a hundred times. Lily bumped me with her nose letting me know she was ready to be done, so I turned back to her and loosened her cinch a bit before pulling the reigns over her head.

Leading her out of the ring and towards the barn I found Rick sitting in his truck. The rig was running, and he was leaning out the window. He had obviously remembered something, so I raised my brow and stopped Lily next to where he sat.

"I'm not going to tell Louisa about the baby," he said, "but I think you need to come talk to her."

I wasn't worried about him telling her. I knew they shared everything and she was family too, so I wasn't concerned about her finding out. I nodded, and he waved again before pulling away. The way he had said it, something in his voice had me unable to move, confusion running through me and questions filling my head. Only when the horse bumped me again did I wake from my stupor and finally made our way to the barn to clean up.

<u>Chapter 12</u>

Looking up at the colonial style home, I let myself be comforted by the sight alone. My cousin and his wife lived on the other side of town from me on a quiet four acres that sat back from the road. The lawns were immaculate and, obviously, Rick's crew had been there this week since all the mulch was fresh. No signs of the tough winter showed here.

Grabbing the pies I had made that afternoon, I hopped out of Kyle's truck and went through the garage to enter the house. The smell of homemade lasagna and garlic bread hit me the minute I stepped over the threshold. Louisa was buzzing around the kitchen, and I could hear the local evening news blaring from the living room. I knew if I walked that far I would find Rick sitting on the couch with a beer in hand unwinding and catching up on the weekly weather.

"Samantha!" she exclaimed with the excitement of a five-year-old when I sat the desserts on the counter and caught her attention.

Before I could return her greeting, I was mushed against her curvy frame in a fierce bear hug. The scent of roses wafted into my nostrils causing tears to sting my eyes. She had worn the same perfume my entire life, and it was one of those fragrances that always brought memories of her to the forefront. I'm not sure how I had gotten so lucky to have her and Rick in my life, but I was eternally grateful for them.

"Hi Lou," I finally managed to get out.

Finding the Way Back
Marcie Shumway

She fussed over me a bit as she released me and quickly put me to work setting the table with four plates. I gave her a questioning glance, but she clucked something about taking the bread out of the oven before it burned. Letting the routine of putting things out relax me, I got the table ready and went back for the large pitcher of water and jug of milk I knew would be in the refrigerator. Louisa had never allowed alcohol at the table unless it was pizza night. She ruled her kitchen with an iron fist, and I adored her for it.

Just as we finished bringing things to the table, Rick came into the kitchen trailed by another man that I would guess was only a few years older than I was. It wasn't seeing someone else there that surprised me, the two of them were always taking in "strays." It was the sadness that filled the man's face that caught me off guard. Most of it was hidden behind a scruffy beard, but his green eyes were red-rimmed and held a pain I couldn't describe. My heart literally ached for him.

We sat down to eat, and within minutes I found out all about their new friend and all of his pain. Brent McAllister had been hired by Rick after a chance meeting at the local hardware store. He had recently moved to Maine to escape memories and move forward with his life. The man had lost his high school sweetheart, his wife, just six short months ago to cancer. Along with their unborn child that they hadn't known she was carrying until after her death. I fought the urge to wrap the poor man in my arms to comfort him while tears filled my eyes as he told his story.

When the meal was finished, Rick and Brent headed out to the garage to do a few things. I really think it was just an excuse so Lou could talk to me, but I was appreciative of

64

the space so I could compose myself. We did dishes in silence, and it wasn't until we were sitting back down at the table with cups of tea did she finally let out what was on her mind.

"Rick said you needed to tell me something," she offered.

Without preamble, I launched into the story of my losing my baby and the struggles Kyle and I were having. Her hand came over to cover mine, and the tears from earlier now streamed freely down my face. I told her of my fears of being a bad mother and of never being able to carry a baby to term. I also told her that I was back to seeing Mrs. Briggs again and that my husband was going with me to the appointments.

"Oh my darling," she cooed. "I hate that you are going through this. I wouldn't wish it on my worst enemy."

Her voice, much like Rick's a few days before, had my eyes jumping up to her face from my mug. The sadness in her features was not for me, it was her own. I knew the feeling to my core. Getting up, she motioned for me to stay while she went to the living room. She came back moments later with one picture that she put in front of me before she took her seat back.

It was an ultrasound. I looked at her, and I'm sure she could see the questions shining in my eyes. She simply pointed to the date. That's when I really looked. This wasn't a picture from her pregnancies with Chris or Matt, my cousins. The date was two years prior to them.

"I was twelve weeks. We had thought we were in the clear and had just told our family. I wanted to tell our friends, but something in my gut told me to wait. I'm so glad that I did because the next day I miscarried."

"Oh, Lou!" I cried, covering my mouth with my hand

as fresh tears tracked down my cheeks.

"Something was wrong with the baby, the doctors told me. It wasn't my fault, and it wasn't meant to be, but the first year I wouldn't hear of it. I blamed myself. I had to have done something wrong."

"But you had two healthy babies after that! I know you didn't do anything wrong," I told her gripping her hand tightly in mine.

"Ah, love, I know that. It took a lot of time and heartache for me to realize it. It also took me almost losing my marriage."

"Rick would never have blamed you or left you," I assured her.

"No, however, I almost left him. I couldn't handle the hurt that I had inadvertently caused him. He deserved someone that would give him all the children I knew he desperately wanted."

Sitting back, I shook my head. It was as though she was telling me my own story. All the things she had felt and gone through, I was feeling and I was going through. Funny what our heads will tell us even though our hearts feel something entirely different.

"Samantha, you will get past this and have many children. You will be a stronger person and a better mother because of it. Mourn for your lost baby because you need to, but then you should allow yourself to heal. You and Kyle need to lean on each other. Your love will help you move on."

With the sound of footsteps coming back through the house, she got up, tucking the picture in her back pocket for safe keeping. I excused myself to clean up my face in the bathroom and when I returned the three of them were seated again with the pies and tea. I joined them and quickly found myself laughing as Rick told one of his famous stories about a "surprise" one of his employees received.

The evening wound down, and as I finished my tea, I looked at my cousin and his wife. While they didn't sit overly close, his hand covered hers as he talked. The look on her face as she giggled at something he said was one of pure love and spoke of the longevity of their relationship. When Rick leaned over to kiss her on the cheek, I sighed. Sure, Kyle and I had been together for years, but this was what I wanted for our future. Decades of marriage, children, and never ending love.

I noticed some of the pain lift from Brent's face as well when he watched them together. I hoped it was because he was thinking fondly of his wife and what they shared, or that he could move on and have what they had once again. Before Lou ushered us out the door, she dumped a pie in each of our hands muttering that we were young and could burn the calories quicker than she could. We both chuckled as we walked out because we could hear Rick complaining that she might not want those calories, but he sure as heck did.

"They are such a wonderful couple," Brent said as he opened the door to his Jeep Wrangler and put the pie in the passenger seat.

"They are," I agreed, doing the same. "I hope you will come by and meet my husband when he comes home."

"I will," he replied climbing in and starting it. "Rick speaks highly of him, and I would like to talk to him about picking up a couple head of cattle."

Before he pulled out, I made sure he had both Kyle and my numbers in his cell phone. As I made the short drive home, I thought about everything from the evening. I couldn't imagine the pain Brent had been through and never wanted to. I would be lost without my husband. He was my other half. Then to find out that Louisa and Rick had been through exactly what Kyle and I had. All the events gave me renewed faith in our ability to get past this and soothed the heartache I had had.

Fifteen minutes later I was climbing from my husband's truck, and my phone rang. My heart was full. "Hey, baby."

Chapter 13

"Easy, girl, easy," I crooned to Lily as we made our way around the arena at a steady canter.

I had been working her and Mac daily to get them ready to head to the Conrad's. The lodge was quickly filling with guests because of the upcoming holiday weekend, and the other horses were already starting to arrive. Normally they would already be there, but due to our last two large snow storms, I hadn't been able to start them as early as I would have liked. Karen had assured me the extra week was fine when I told her I wanted more time with the mare. She was still a little hot, and I worried that she would give the inexperienced riders a hard time.

"Let's slow it down," I told her, sitting deeper in the saddle and tugging gently to warn her of what was coming.

The toss of her head should have been my first indication that she was going to misbehave. I thought it was just going to be an "I don't wanna" kind of deal, but I couldn't have been more wrong. The next thing I knew, I was hitting the ground with a solid *thud*. Laying there for a moment, stunned, I watched as she trotted towards the gate where someone was climbing up and over it to come to me. I shook my head to clear it and took an assessment. Nothing was broken, but I'd definitely be sore in the morning. Getting to my feet, I brushed myself off and looked up when the footfall got closer.

"Hey!" I exclaimed. "What are you doing home already?"

"With everything going on I wanted to be home, so

here I am," my husband said, patting his hands over me to make sure I was truly okay.

Stopping his movements with my hands, I jumped in his arms to kiss and hug him for all I was worth. The distance had never bothered me before, yet this time I had felt like I was missing something with him being gone. Maybe with the idea of starting a family, we needed to discuss him being closer to home. I knew he loved his job and I didn't want to take that away from him. However, I wasn't going to raise a child primarily by myself. It had been brought up before about him going down to Dane Iron Company. It was an hour drive twice a day versus him being gone three weeks at a time, that worked for me.

"Let's go catch her, so you can get back on," he chuckled, pulling away after giving me one last kiss on the forehead.

I moaned and followed him over to the gate where Lily was waiting patiently. Evidently, since I wasn't on her back, she felt it was time to go back to the barn. Shaking my head at her, I grabbed the reins and led her to the mounting block. Kyle held her head so she didn't try walking off on me while I swung my leg over her. When he knew I was settled into the saddle, he stepped back and leaned against the fence to watch.

"Okay, girlie, let's try this again," I murmured to her.

We moved back out to the rail, and I started the process all over again. We walked for a bit, crossing corner to corner diagonally to toss things up. Once she relaxed, we moved into a trot and continued the same pattern. Finally, I tried the canter again. This time it went off without a hitch. I shook my head as I cooled her off and moved back towards Kyle to take her out of the arena.

"I don't know what to do with her," I said to him,

totally exasperated. "She's never this bad."

"Call Chad and talk to him," Kyle replied, patting my leg to comfort me. "She loves kids, so maybe after a few rides under Chad she will calm down for them."

I shrugged and dismounted, feeling the fall from earlier. The two of us finished taking care of her and did chores in a routine that was comforting. We moved around each other like we were dancing, each predicting the others movements. When we were done, we walked to the house hand-in-hand, and I couldn't have been more content.

The next morning we loaded up Mac and Lily into the trailer and headed over to the Conrad's. I had called Chad the night before, and he was confident that the mare would come out of her naughty behavior in no time. I trusted his judgment, so we decided to bring them over a few days earlier than planned so that he could work with her. I fidgeted the short ride over until Kyle put his hand over mine and squeezed gently. The warmth and weight of his hand calmed me instantly, and I threw him a grateful smile as we pulled into the long drive.

He pulled the truck and trailer past the main building and brought it to a stop next to the barn. I hopped out and made my way to the door of the trailer that was for the tack room. By the time I had gathered both lead lines, Chad and Kyle were at the back of the trailer with the doors open waiting for me.

Between the three of us, we easily got the horses unloaded. They were used to the trip since they had been doing it for years, so neither one of them batted an eyelash when they were off. Chad took Lily from me and motioned for Kyle to continue forward to put Mac in the paddock with a couple of other horses. It was then that I noticed there was a saddle on the fence of the arena and a bridle hanging from a post.

"Before you two head out, I want to see how she is acting," he told me as we stopped next to the tack.

My friend got the horse ready while I strapped on the helmet that my husband brought out to me. When she was ready, I walked her out and made sure her girth was tight before hoping on. She didn't make it easy, side stepping and walking off as she had been doing at home. Chad finally came over and held her so that I could get on her.

Lily pulled all the quirks she had been. The only thing that she didn't do was unseat me. By the time I brought her back to where Chad and Kyle were leaning on the fence, I was beyond frustrated. Our friend's brow was furrowed in thought when I stopped in front of them, and he motioned for me to get down. I happily obliged, handing him the reins and removing my helmet while I leaned on the fence beside my husband.

When Chad mounted without any problems, my frustration grew. She was a gem as he put her through her paces, walk, trot, and canter. Kyle felt me shifting uneasily next to him and grabbed my hand in his to squeeze it and calm me. I couldn't believe she was behaving so well for him when she had been a complete brat for me the past few weeks. Tears pricked my eyes. I couldn't even ride my own horses anymore on top of everything else.

"Well," Chad said as he brought her over to us and dismounted, "I would say she is feeding off you and whatever you have going on personally."

My stomach dropped at the same time that Kyle gripped my hand tighter. As long as I had had horses, how had I not realized? Mac had been fine, but Lily was much more sensitive to her rider. She picked up on everything.

Finding the Way Back
Marcie Shumway

She was taking advantage of the fact that I was distracted and knew that I wasn't myself.

Stepping away from the gate I let go of Kyle and cupped Lily's head in my hands. Kissing her velvety fur, I whispered my apology to her and giggled when she nudged me with her nose in return. Chad let me take her in the barn to untack her and brush her down before she was turned out with the others.

While the guys closed up the trailer, I watched Mac and Lily. It was better that they were here being used by the campers this summer. I still had Remi and Fighter at home to ride. At least here, they would be loved and given all the attention they could handle. Maybe when they came home in late fall, I would have a better handle on things.

"Don't blame yourself," Kyle comforted as we left ten minutes later. "We have a lot going on."

"I know, but I've had her for more than ten years," I reminded him. "I should know what's bothering her better than anyone."

"This is exactly why I came home without mentioning it to you," he murmured softly. "You need me."

"I do," I whispered back.

"That's also why I had an interview with Dane two weeks ago," he told me with a slight grin. "I start with them in a couple months."

Chapter 14

"Why do we watch chick flicks if we know they are going to make us cry?" Lisa asked wiping tears from her cheeks.

"Cause we are all suckers for a love story," I chuckled as I got up and gathered our dirty ice cream mugs.

"I'll help," Skye said putting Eric in Lisa's arms and gathering the remaining dishes.

"I hope the guys are having fun," I commented as we deposited everything on the sideboard in the kitchen.

"I'm sure they are," she laughed, "based on the text messages we have been receiving.

The guys were having their bachelor "party" for Chad. They had gone four-wheeling for the day and had rented one of the Conrad's cabins for the night. For the last hour, all three of us had been getting drunk texts from them. It was highly entertaining and had put us in stitches despite the crying over the movie. I was so grateful that the six of us had each other.

"How have you been?" Skye asked as she filled the sink with warm water and soap.

"Better," I told her honestly as I grabbed a towel to dry after she washed. "The counseling has helped a lot."

"Are you back with Mrs. Briggs?" she questioned handing me a washed and rinsed mug.

"We both are," I answered, quickly drying it and putting it in the waiting open cupboard. "It hasn't been easy digging up stuff I thought had been long put behind me, but it gives me a lot of insight as to the reasons I feel the way I do."

"I'm so glad. You always seemed to feel better after you saw her back when we were growing up. I even started going to her after I returned home."

"You?!" I exclaimed nearly dropping the silverware in my hand.

"Yeah. After everything with Steve, I started having panic attacks. I knew I needed to see someone and I remembered how highly you spoke of her."

Tears pricked my eyes, gosh I cried a lot lately, "I'm so happy she was able to help you."

"She was the final piece," she said, putting her wet hand on mine. "Coming home to all of you was the best thing for me."

I hugged her, hard. Before we turned into blubbery messes again, we finished what we were doing and made our way back out to the living room. Lisa was crashed on the couch with little Eric asleep on her chest. Before we woke her, we did the one thing only good friends would do, and that was take a million pictures. Skye smoothly moved her son without waking him, and while she put him in his carrier, I nudged Lisa.

After multiple assurances that I would receive text messages when they both arrived home, the ladies left. I did a quick night check on all the animals and was locking up when my phone rang. Sliding my shoes off near the door, I swiped across to the screen to answer it as I made my way upstairs.

"I don't want you to get pregnant," came Kyle's greeting, or lack thereof.

"Kyle? What are you talking about?" I stammered, dropping down on the bed in our room.

"That came out wrong," was his slurred response. "I

meant, that you shouldn't get pregnant."

"I shouldn't?" I asked, pinching the bridge of my nose with my fingers and taking a deep breath. Drunk texts could be funny, yet the drunk phone calls never seemed to be.

"You know what I mean!" he accused, cursing under his breath as I heard him hit something.

"Are you okay?"

"Yeah, stupid bed moved."

"Uh huh...." I drew out, trying my hardest not to giggle as he was obviously trying to have a serious conversation with me despite his inebriation.

"I'm scared, Sam," he whispered all slurring gone. "What if we lose another one?"

"We will get through it together," I assured him.

"What if I lose you and the baby?"

I was speechless. I knew I had to tread lightly, so he didn't do something stupid in his drunken state, but I hadn't expected to hear that. Where had that come from? Had the miscarriage done the same damage to him that it did to me emotionally?

"Kyle, I'm not going anywhere," I told him. "They will have to take me kicking and screaming."

"I'm not sure if I can do this. If I can be a dad. What if I screw the kid up?"

"That's why there are two of us, babe," I reminded him, chuckling.

"How can you be so sure of everything?"

"I'm not," I scoffed. "I'm scared too."

"Good."

"Yeah, at least we can screw up the kid together," I joked.

"You'll be an *ama*-zing mother," he informed me

dragging out the amazing part.

I grinned hearing the smile and dream-like sound of his voice. "And you will be the best dad ever."

"Samantha Hart, I love you."

"Kyle Hart, I love you too."

"We'll start trying tomorrow as soon as I get home," he giggled, yes, giggled like a little boy saying something he wasn't supposed to. "You'd better be ready for me!"

"I'm always ready for you," I laughed.

A couple more *I love you's* later, and I was finally able to hang up the phone. I couldn't help the smile that graced my lips as I changed into pajamas and crawled into bed. Settling in on Kyle's side, I inhaled the scent of him that still clung to his pillow. Warmth and peace filled me to the core.

As much I didn't like that Kyle was scared about us trying to have a baby, it brought some comfort to know I wasn't the only one with fears and trepidation about the whole thing. It finally felt like we were getting somewhere with counseling and communication. Now, if only my body would catch up with my heart and do its part.

Chapter 15

"Are you sure you'll be all set?" Skye asked for the millionth time as I removed a sleeping Eric from his carrier.

"We'll be fine," I assured her snuggling the baby against my chest. "It's not like we haven't watched him before and you are only a phone call away."

Skye had mentioned wanting some alone time with her husband, so I had volunteered Kyle and myself to take Eric for the night. I don't think she had really thought things through. I figured it would be a great opportunity for us to get a feel for having an infant in the house and they would only be a short distance away if we didn't feel we could handle it.

"Sweetheart," JJ crooned, pulling Skye against his side with one arm, "he'll be fine. It's one night, and you can call Sam all you want."

She turned the stink eye on her husband causing him to back up with his hands in the air and a chuckle. Kyle rolled his eyes beside me, and she gave him a swat in the stomach for his actions. I handed her son back to her for a couple of last minute kisses. Assuring her everything would be okay, I took him back, and JJ ushered her out the door.

"Wow," Kyle sighed as he shut the door behind them.

"I think she was doing this for us more than herself," I told him as I handed him the baby and took the rest of Eric's things upstairs to our bedroom.

"Why would she do it for us?" he asked following me.

Finding the Way Back
Marcie Shumway

"She knows we have been having some reservations about things and wanted us to see how gratifying it can be to be parents," I said putting the bags down next to the Pack and Play that was set up as his crib for the night. "I just don't think she realized it would be her first night away from him."

"Maybe we should take him back," he stammered as the baby started to fuss in his arms.

"Everything will be fine," I promised him taking the bundle from him and checking his diaper. "It looks like you get your first shot at changing too!"

Teaching my husband how to change a baby was an experience in itself. I had babysat as a teenager, and I had refreshed my memory spending time with Skye and Eric. I couldn't contain my laughter each time Kyle would gag from the smell as he cleaned him up. The baby had spared no expense on his first messy diaper with us. I didn't know how he had managed to keep it all in and not get it on his clothes.

When we were done, we went back downstairs. The boys settled into the living room while I went to the kitchen to finish up the homemade pizza I was making for supper. I was just putting it in the oven when my phone signaled a text message. It was Skye checking in. Laughing, I sent her a reply.

Grabbing chips and a couple of sodas, I made my way to the living room and was going to mention it to Kyle when I was stopped in my tracks. He sat on the couch with his knees up, and Eric was leaning against his legs. The two seemed to be engaged in a very serious conversation. Kyle held Eric's little hands in his work-hardened ones and was whispering to him. The baby watched him intently, his body a constant wiggle

Finding the Way Back
Marcie Shumway

I hadn't been kidding when I had told my husband he would be a great father. When I watched him with our animals, the patience and love he showed them, I knew it. Seeing him with the infant just solidified it. I couldn't wait to see him hold our own baby that way. Maybe it was time for us to finally have that conversation.

Despite the drunk phone call a few nights before, we hadn't talked again about trying to have another baby. Heck, he hadn't even touched me other than a hug or light kiss. Part of the reason I had practically begged Skye to take Eric was in the hopes of triggering him to either talk about it or turn to me physically. By the looks of it, it was the right thing to do.

"You know you can put him down," I told Kyle a half hour later as we ate and he still had Eric held against his chest with his free arm.

"I like holding him," he responded simply, an ear-to-ear smile on his face.

I sent Skye a picture of the two of them lounging on the couch after dinner before I went back to clean up the kitchen. My smile was just as big after watching them. Once I was done, I went back to the living room. Kyle was still telling Eric stories, and he was still looking at my husband as though he held the world. It was adorable.

Crawling into bed a few hours later, Eric asleep in the Pack and Play, Kyle spooned up to my back and wrapped me in his arms. I twined my arms with his and pulled him as close as humanly possible. The warmth of his body against mine made me feel safe and lulled me instantly into a deep sleep.

I'm not sure how long I had been out, but suddenly I was up and beside the Pack and Play picking up a fussing baby. I had gotten up so quick that Kyle hadn't even had a

Finding the Way Back
Marcie Shumway

chance to roll over and he was on the closest side of the
bed. I had never thought of myself as a light sleeper but
evidently, my motherly instincts kicked in. Checking his
diaper I found him dry, so I tucked him in the crook of my
arm and talked to him while we went downstairs to warm a
bottle.

Noticing that my husband hadn't followed me, I took
Eric into the guest room so that we didn't bother him. I
clicked on the small desk light before sitting down in the old
rocker that was beside the window overlooking the
pastures. Through the open window, a warm June breeze
could be felt, and I could hear the horses snorting and
moving. Singing softly to Eric, I pushed off my toe and set
the chair into slow motion rocking.

Watching the baby as he worked the nipple on the
bottle, I counted each little digit wrapped around one of
mine and brushed another across his perfect little cheek. His
eyes started to close with each back and forth of the chair
causing my heart to swell. He was a perfect combination of
both of our friends. I couldn't wait until I was looking down
into a face that was both mine and Kyle's. His eyes, my
smile.

"You are a pro," I heard Kyle whisper from the door.

I looked up and found the same look on his face that
I'm sure had been on mine earlier in the evening when I had
been watching him. The love I saw there made my blood
heat up, and the sight of his arms crossed across his chest
had my uterus singing a tune. He moved through the room
and put a hand on each arm of the chair, face to face with
me. The kiss he placed on my lips was light, sweet, and filled
with so much promise.

"I think it's time we tried again to have one of our
own."

Chapter 16

The fourth of July dawned beautiful, hot, and the perfect day for a wedding. There wasn't a cloud in the sky, and I was extremely grateful that Lisa had picked dresses for us that in a light and breathable material. I stood in Lisa's bathroom putting long waves in my hair with the curling iron, laughing every time I heard one of the girl's curse while they were working on the bride's hair. Skye and Morgan, Chad's sister, were trying to duplicate some intricate up-do Lisa had found in a magazine.

Chad and Lisa had decided to have the ceremony at their new home with just a few friends and family, the reception would follow at the Conrad's lodge with the guests there. The trail ride we all normally did with the guests on the holiday would ride out the next day instead. It was going to be a busy week, but I wouldn't trade it for the world.

"Where did your mom end up?" I asked Morgan when I finished my make-up and brought all my stuff out of the bathroom.

"She's keeping my mom busy, so she doesn't drive me crazy," Lisa told me.

I chuckled causing her to stick her tongue out at me. It was no secret that Lisa and her mother, Mary, had a trying relationship. Karen had been the one to step in for all of us. After I had zipped my bag, I straightened and looked at my friend. Jess Wing, the photographer, was snapping away with her camera and Lisa was absolutely glowing.

Her hair was done up with just a few tendrils coming

down the sides of her face, and she was still clad in a robe, yet I had never seen someone so beautiful. She caught me looking at her and sent me a smile as she worked with Jess on some shots of the dress and of her getting ready to put it on. It wasn't long before she motioned us over to help her. Between the four of us, we were able to help her get it on and zipped without messing up her hair.

Not long after she was dressed, her mom came bursting in the door. Tears were shed, and the activity level picked up. It wouldn't be long now before Lisa Brown became Lisa Conrad. I can't say that I ever saw that one coming. At least not until I had seen them together at Skye and JJ's wedding. For a couple that had been friends most of their lives and together for a very short time, they were meant to be. They just worked.

"Will you do my makeup?" Morgan asked, breaking me out of my own thoughts.

"Of course," I replied grabbing her bag from her and following her into the bathroom.

As I put foundation on her upturned face and listened to her talk about her first year of college, I sighed. Things were changing. I remembered when Chad's sister was a child following us around clad in overalls with pigtails and now she was in college. It was a hard pill to swallow. I highlighted her bright brown eyes to make them *pop* with her long brown waves. Topping it all off with a little pink on her cheeks and lips. She was definitely growing into a stunning young woman.

"It's time to go ladies!" Morgan announced when she checked her phone as we re-entered Lisa's bedroom.

Pandemonium ensued. Lisa's stepfather, Craig, came in to walk her outside and to her groom. I could see her face flash white under her make-up from the nerves, however, I knew once she saw Chad all would be forgotten. Morgan, Karen, and Mary all went out ahead of us to sit with the family. Skye and I each gave Lisa a kiss on the cheek and headed out towards the kitchen and the French doors that would lead us out to the backyard.

Chad, JJ, and Kyle all stood at the edge of the tree line, the same place where he had proposed, with the justice of the peace. All three were dressed in new black Carhartt pants and white button-up shirts. Damn were we lucky women! I heard the music start that signaled us to walk down the short aisle between the chairs. Chad gave us each a smile, and I blew a kiss in my husband's direction as we got closer. Just as we found our places, the wedding march started, and everyone stood.

I knew the minute that Lisa's eyes met Chad's, the nerves on her face melted away and tears filled his. The love between the two was obvious to anyone there. I felt my own eyes fill and shared a teary smile with Skye when she turned to look at me. It was hard to believe that nine months ago we were watching her and JJ say their vows and cut their cake to find out that they were expecting little Eric.

The ceremony was short and sweet. When it was over, we all piled into our vehicles and headed over to the lodge. Duncan and Karen had left ahead of us to make sure everything was ready for the wedding guests. Kyle helped me down from the truck so my dress didn't ride up, and we went in.

The large dining room had been cleared and set up just as it had for our other friends. It was hard to believe that now all of us had been married and celebrated here. A buffet was set up against one wall and near the windows was the wedding cake. We beelined for the head table to put down my purse and our bag with our change of clothes for later. Once everyone was there, Karen directed the wedding party to grab our food first.

Before I knew it, the first dance, father-daughter dance, and mother-son dance were all done. The girls dragged me out, and we danced to songs that were from back when we were in high school. It felt good to be out there with them laughing and kicking up our heels. I was just about to take a break when a slow song came on, and I was stumbling into a pair of strong familiar arms.

"Hello there, beautiful lady," he murmured in my ear as we swayed to the beat. "Like the song?"

"Hey you," I returned putting my head on his chest, "I do. Sounds like something we danced to on our wedding day."

"You remember," he gushed with a laugh. "How are you feeling?"

"Good," I assured him squeezing my arms where they rested around his neck.

Aunt Flo had visited the previous morning, but this time when the tears had come, Kyle had been there to pick me up. We had cried together and talked about the future. It had been just what I had needed to move past it and just what we had needed as a couple to keep going forward.

"We'll get there," he told me as we finished dancing. "I promise."

"Even if we don't, I'll be just fine as long as I have you."

Watching Chad and Lisa and Skye and JJ later on that night, I couldn't have been happier. All of my friends were in wonderful relationships, married, children. Their future was finally headed in the same direction that ours was. It felt good to see their dreams coming true and the contentment they had with their lives after all the trials and tribulations. I

Finding the Way Back
Marcie Shumway

could only hope that ours would, as well.

Chapter 17

It was hard to believe that it was already the middle of August. After Lisa and Chad's wedding, July had become a blur. I had been so busy helping at the lodge along with working at our own farm that I didn't know where the month had gone. I hadn't realized it was over until Kyle had reminded me that he was officially home for good and would now be around every night.

Silly man, I thought to myself as I finished up the dinner dishes. I could hear him talking to the horses through the open kitchen window that was letting in the warm summer breeze. He was checking on them one last time before we settled in for the night. It was his way of getting out of doing dishes, but the sound of his voice as he crooned to them filled my soul.

Turning to hang the towel I had been using to dry my hands, I caught the calendar hanging on the wall out of the corner of my eye. I had to do a double-take. It was the 12th. I hadn't had a period since the wedding, six weeks ago. Stopping, I took a deep breath.

"Kyle!!!!"

Seconds later my husband came rushing in the door, out of breath and his eyes taking me in to make sure I was okay. I shook my head at him to let him know nothing was wrong at the same time that tears filled my eyes. Without asking anything, he came over and wrapped me in his arms, still heaving slightly from the exertion. I hugged his solid, warm body fiercely before leaning back slightly to look at his face.

"I'm late," I whispered.

His head snapped back at the comment, and I could see him searching my face for an explanation. I saw him look at the calendar over my head, he knew my cycle as well as I did these days, and his eyes widened when he too realized the date. Kyle's hands came up to cup my face, and the kiss he planted on my lips was supportive and filled with love. It said we would be okay, no matter what happened.

"Do you have any tests?" he asked.

"Yep," I replied still whispering, "but I'm scared to take one."

"I'm right here with you this time, baby," he reminded me.

I followed him up to our bathroom and leaned against the doorframe to watch him as he dug around in the linen closet. I couldn't help but smile at him when he turned around and handed me the box. Some men would shy away from this part, yet mine was stepping up to the plate in a big way. I knew he wanted this as much as I did, but he was putting it all aside to take care of me. Kissing him on the cheek, I took the test from him and shut the door so I could do what I needed to.

Did I say the two-week wait was the worst? Yeah, more like the two-minute wait is. I had somehow forgotten the torture of the lines. Will it show one line or two? Kyle paced uneasily beside our bed that I was now laying back on with my feet on the floor. I didn't even move when the timer on his phone went off. I just closed my eyes and concentrated on my breathing.

"Want me to check it?" he asked, uncertainty in his voice.

I nodded. I couldn't look. My stomach was threatening to send dinner back up, and I put my hand on it to help steady it. I had done this step more times than I could count without him. It was his turn. I heard his boot clad feet head into our bathroom and come back, then silence.

I laid there for what felt like forever. My ears strained to hear even a change in his breathing or shift of his body, but nothing. I felt tears escape my eyes and roll down my face to the comforter. It was negative, again.

Finally, I opened my eyes and sat up. When I finished wiping my face, I looked up at Kyle. He stood looking at the stick with a stupid, silly grin on his face. Confusion and mild excitement raced through me. It couldn't be? Was I pregnant?

"Kyle?!" I screeched breaking him from his trance.

"We did it!" he exclaimed fist punching the air like a teenager and pulling me to my feet.

That night Kyle held nothing back as he showed me how much he loved and treasured me, from the inside out. The next morning I took another test, just to make sure. It still didn't seem real when I saw the two pink lines pop up in the circle. They were there, and they were strong, nothing faint about them.

"The results aren't going to change no matter how many times you take it," Kyle chuckled at me as I continued to stare at the two sticks.

"I know, but with everything we've been through it just seems surreal," I told him.

"We just had to be patient," he informed me, coming up to wrap his arms around me and place his hands on my still flat stomach.

"Says the man that watches the calendar and wants me to take a test when I'm a day late," I responded with a laugh.

Finding the Way Back
Marcie Shumway

Leaning down to nip at my neck, he pulled his arms from me and slapped my butt to get me moving. We had decided we would take care of the animals together, grab breakfast, and head to the Conrad's. It was a beautiful summer day, and there were always things to do with the campers. Sitting around wouldn't do either of us any good. Though, we did agree that we wouldn't share with anyone until we had confirmation from the doctor.

Two weeks later, we had it. Walking out of the brick building this time had a much happier feel. I couldn't stop looking at the ultrasound I held in my hand. Granted, I had done this before, only to lose the precious cargo I had been carrying. This time felt different. I felt better, I felt stronger. Kyle squeezed my hand and tugged me towards the truck. The smile on his face ran ear-to-ear and hadn't disappeared since the night we had taken the original test.

When I hopped into the truck, it took all I had not to do a happy dance. I was elated. It didn't matter what happened at this point. My marriage was growing stronger by the day, and now we had a little one to look forward to. Looking over at my husband as he maneuvered us out of the parking lot, I put my hand on his arm. Turning to look at me, he picked up my hand in one of his and kissed the back of it.

"Stop at Doc's," I told him looking down at the picture briefly. "We need provisions."

He never questioned me because he knew exactly what I was thinking. Dropping a quick text to Lisa to tell her and JJ to meet us, we grabbed food and coffee for everyone and headed to the lodge. When we pulled in and Kyle parked, I froze. Maybe I shouldn't be telling them so soon. After all, I was only eight weeks along. We weren't even out of the "safe" zone yet.

"Stop overthinking this," Kyle whispered in my ear

leaning over the center console. "They are our support system. If – big *IF* – something happens, they will help us pick up the pieces."

That had been just what I needed to hear. Walking into the lodge, I stopped and took everything in. Karen, Duncan, and Skye were at the front desk looking over the check-in book while Chad stood off to the side holding Eric, carrying on a one-sided conversation as the baby watched him with big eyes. I turned when I heard JJ and Lisa come up behind us and leaned into my friend when she wrapped her arm around my shoulders. This was my family, and I couldn't have asked for better.

We took the bags and coffees outside to the farmer's porch that wrapped around the main building. I waved for Karen and Duncan to join us when they tried to duck away and looped my arm through Morgan's to make sure she joined us as well. I wanted them all to know that our dreams finally seemed to be coming true.

"So, what do we owe this breakfast to?" Skye asked when everyone was settled in. "Not that this is anything new, but Kyle should be at work."

I laughed at her pointing out the obvious. We had all gathered for breakfast on work days countless times, with or without Kyle depending on his schedule out of state. Now that he was working closer to home and had a normal nine-to-five, he wasn't able to join us unless we did it on the weekends. I loved that she never beat around the bush.

"Maybe we just wanted to see you all," Kyle teased, turning slightly and making me stifle a giggle when I saw the ultrasound peaking out of his back pocket.

"What is that?!" Lisa screeched reaching for the picture, leave it to her to be checking out my husband's butt.

"Oh my god!" Karen gasped, her hand clasping over her mouth.

"Is that yours?!" JJ asked, wincing at how it sounded and earning him a slap on the back of the head from his wife.

"Ours, yes," Kyle answered. His grin seemed to grow bigger if that was even possible.

Our friends jumped up and cheered, hugged and kissed us. Love flowed, and my fears were eased. The decision to tell them had been the right one. They would keep us up if anything went wrong and they would celebrate with us when things were right.

"I'm so happy for you, Sam," Skye told me as she pulled back from our hug. "You will be an amazing mother. You have so much love to give. That baby will never, never feel the way you did for so long."

<u>Chapter 18</u>

Approximately 8 months later...

"She's perfect," Brent murmured as he inspected each of the baby's little fingers and little toes.

"She is," I agreed, pulling my feet underneath me on the couch to get more comfortable.

Madison Rose Hart had been born a week early, weighing in at 7 pounds 8 ounces and was 20 inches long. I was in hard labor for three hours, and everything had gone smoothly. She was a blondie like her momma and was the perfect baby. We were so in love with her, and I often found myself just watching her sleep so that I didn't miss a moment of her tiny life.

"I can't tell you how happy I am for you guys," he told me looking up as he cradled Maddie in his lap.

"Thank you," I replied leaning towards him and setting my hand on his arm. "I know this hasn't been easy for you. We appreciate all the help."

Part way through my pregnancy I became doctor-ordered bed ridden. For someone like me who is very active, I was crushed. Until I realized it meant I could sleep and read all the time, two of my favorite things outside of my animals and my husband. Brent had become a fixture on our farm aiding in chores, riding the horses, and keeping Kyle sane.

He'd struggled as we had all gotten closer. One day I finally had Kyle send him to our room so I could figure out what was going on with him. He tried to avoid it but finally admitted that he was scared. He cared about me like a sister and was afraid for me and the baby after what had happened to his wife. Once she had been born, I had seen the difference. The weight lifted. Now he was working on enjoying her like the rest of us.

"It wasn't a problem," he assured me. "You guys have all welcomed me into your group so quickly. I needed that, and I didn't even know it."

"They are a pretty amazing group," I said, getting up and looking out the living room window.

This was the first time we had all gotten together since the previous fall. It was an abnormally warm late April day, so we had decided a cookout was in order. Skye and Lisa sat in Adirondack chairs on our farmer's porch while Morgan sat playing with Eric at their feet. Kyle worked the grill and Chad and JJ stood near him, all three engaged in some conversation that had them laughing and nudging each other. The whole scene warmed my heart.

Hearing Maddie begin to fuss, I turned around to head towards Brent. He gave her back to me all too quickly when she looked like she was ready to wail. I laughed at the expression on his face and took her upstairs to feed her while he headed out to join the others. Settling into the old rocker now in our bedroom, I set us into motion while I nursed her.

These were the most precious of moments. The ones that I wanted to bottle up and keep forever. We had struggled the past two years between the miscarriage and trying to get pregnant. I wasn't sure if I was ready to go through it all again, but looking down at the angelic face filling her belly, I was grateful we had at least gotten one. I had experienced pregnancy, childbirth, and having my own child. Even if we didn't have any others, our family felt complete.

Finding the Way Back
Marcie Shumway

A half hour later, I was back outside with everyone. Maddie was wrapped up and tucked in the crook of my arm while I brought a few things for our meal from the house. Seeing what I was doing, Lisa and Skye immediately hopped up to help. Before long the table was set, and Kyle was shutting down the grill and carrying over burgers and hot dogs. As soon as he sat them down, he plucked the baby from my arms and motioned for me to eat. I smiled and filled a plate while he cuddled with her.

Once my belly was full, I sat back and looked around. There were multiple conversations going on, and people seemed to be thoroughly enjoying the day. I was so lucky to have the wonderful friends that I did. Ones that loved me for who I was and that did so without reservation.

"Everything okay?" Kyle asked dropping down on the bench beside me, Maddie still tucked safely in his arms.

"It's perfect," I informed him, gently stroking my daughter's tiny hand and kissing his cheek softly.

And it truly was. It had been a tough couple of years for us, but we had made it through. We had survived a miscarriage, bumps in our marriage, and, for the first time, uncertainty about our future. As I took in those around me, my heart swelled. Thanks to the love and support of my husband and all of them, I had found my way back.

Finding the Way Back
Marcie Shumway

Finding the Way Back
Marcie Shumway

Finding the Way Back
Marcie Shumway

Finding the Way Back
Marcie Shumway

Finding the Way Back
Marcie Shumway

Finding the Way Back
Marcie Shumway

Finding the Way Back
Marcie Shumway

Finding the Way Back
Marcie Shumway

Finding the Way Back
Marcie Shumway

Finding the Way Back
Marcie Shumway

www.ingramcontent.com/pod-product-compliance
Lightning Source LLC
Chambersburg PA
CBHW070504130626
46555CB00003B/1151